THE MAN IN M

Often referred to as a young Mar
is an author and playwright fast growi
poetically sinister storytelling.

In July 2016, Anthony's debut pla
premiered to a standing ovation at Be
as 'One of the best plays to visit the venue,' the production returned by
popular demand for a second smash hit run in 2017.

'The Man in My Footsteps' is a thrilling novella of the darker, more
disturbing kind and is Anthony's first book.

His acclaimed works have attracted the attention of various news
and media outlets such as the BBC while earning him the admiration of
highly established industry peers.

Anthony can also be heard discussing his work regularly on live
radio.

He resides in Bedfordshire, England.

Twitter: @byAnthonyLowery

What readers say

THE MAN IN MY FOOTSTEPS

Ian,
Massive Happy Birthday.
Here's to you!
Cheers

ANTHONY LOWERY

The Man in My Footsteps/ Anthony Lowery. -- 2nd ed.

ISBN 978-0-9955417-0-2

CONTENTS

ACKNOWLEDGEMENTS

I would like to thank my sister Carey for reading *The Man in My Footsteps* one chapter at a time as I wrote it, and telling me what she thought.

My family deserve huge thanks for all their love and support to date - Mum, Abbie, Corrina, Grandma Abigail and Grandad Arthur.

Further thanks and appreciation to those good folks who so kindly lent me their ears and their expertise – Alanna McClure and Stuart Moore.

And special thanks to Josh Gold and Emily Williams, for labours above and beyond the call...

For Nan.

Who listened. And loved.

And always carried.

To you, my friend,

Is it me or has the world fallen into madness? I can't see my
love, nor can I feel her close; if you find her before I do, tell
her that I am looking. I ache as if there can be no glory, but
you laugh as if there's a hopeful end to this story.

Let me tell you a secret, but promise you'll keep it
between you and me. A man is a fickle child in disguise.
When he moves forward, he finds loss and fears what he
found.

When that day came for me - the day when my world
collapsed, like it will for you - there were things that I never
asked her, but how they ruin me now. I scrambled over
faces and clambered over walls, desperately reaching for the
pure sky, but ahead there was just darkness and everything
behind me had died.

Some advice for you now: come in from the callous confines of your mind, because guilt is all you'll find there and guilt is wasteful; guilt was my poison that brewed in the obscurity of my perception. But for me, tomorrow will always come and tomorrow may well bring the sunshine again.

As you walk with me now, I'll stumble through the years, one day to the next, caught in the gap between rapture and damnation; won't you help me answer the questions that lay ignorant beneath these stars?

I ran through the vacant passages of my mind and hid in the deepest, darkest corner of my soul, just to keep the fire from burning within.

When the tempest settles and it's time for my final boarding call, I mustn't forget about the rope I tied around my neck.

So, come. Gather 'round and see it my way.

Yours faithfully,
William Hardy

CHAPTER ONE

A Familiar Stranger

He dug his own grave long before he died but not before his heart stopped beating. He kept death's cold embrace waiting, for he knew that he was never going to rest in peace.

18 July, 1908 was a dry Saturday afternoon. The sun shone a purple colour through the flowery treetops and a sweet smell hung in the air like a cloud. Children were playing and soaking up the summer day while young lovers displayed their affections with all the innocence you might expect from a child. Above, there were forest birds chirping limericks from the branches that stretched out into the open space. To the east was a sun-kissed river that ran parallel to the park for a distance before veering off out of sight. Rolling hills, in every shade of green, obscured the horizon and a single shade of blue coloured in the clear

sky. Playthings and wild growth plotted the rest of the park; shabby shrubs wrestled for daylight and a variety of trees towered, but with a degree of consideration so as not to blot out the sun as it shone down from its jealous sky.

William watched the day unfold from the boundaries of a timeworn bench, battered and stained by the seasons on an eternal loop. It was the same bench that he had sat on for years, perfectly positioned so as to get a view of the entire green without being too far, nor too close, to its often populated centre; not that there was anything wrong with that, of course, he just rather liked to observe from a distance like a painter studying his subject.

Finding beauty in the everyday was something of a hobby for William. Just yesterday he had watched a single leaf ride a gust of the wind like a canoe rides the rapids. It pleased him to get lost in the simple pleasantries of life and he never had to look too far in the charming village of Mane to find something beautiful, as Mane is in itself, quite beautiful; although it wasn't always that way, as the village had only blossomed when William reached his late teens.

Tucked away in an innocuous corner of our emerald land, Mane is a secluded idyll of rural predictability and neighbourly conformity - a sanctuary of all things tedious and distasteful. It is a rather small place, but never too small for the wants of its tight-knit community.

Seated on the opposite side of the park to William was an elderly lady, whose time-honoured appearance suggested she was just past seventy. She was cocooned in layers of clothing, matching in colour, taking shelter from the occasional gust of chilling wind that no one else had seemed to notice. William had seen her in the park many times before, but an elderly gentleman usually accompanied her. The couple would just sit, hand-in-hand, for as long as William sat opposite.

Although he was content where he was, firmly couched in his skin with the pleasant thoughts of the day keeping him company, William found himself strangely compelled to offer the lady companionship.

With a strong sense of moral obligation, he rose to his feet and began to make his way across the park. After being sat for so long, William was suddenly aware of the weight of his own feet; he hoisted them one in front of the other in some jagged manner as if he had forgotten how to walk entirely.

His path to the woman was indirect so as not to disturb anybody, yet he rather felt he was doing that anyway just by stirring.

As his muscle memory woke up and he began to remember how to walk, William felt a strange urge to move quicker, so as to get across the park as soon as he could. His feet chose their own pace, swiftly treading over the soft, grass-covered dirt as if this woman leaving before he got there would be the worst thing in the world.

The chill that he hadn't noticed until now stole his breath for a moment but was soon returned to him unharmed.

'Excuse me, do you mind if I join you?' William asked, as he arrived at the woman's bench unnoticed.

William thought it only polite to ask, although he didn't know what he would have done if she had said no, especially after he had pulled himself away from the most comfortable spot outside of his own bed.

Without a second's thought, the lady turned to William and gave him the quietest of nods.

She was only a little lady, so little that she made the bench appear larger than the others that were dotted around the green. She sat stiff and upright, hands clutching her knees as they gently quaked in the breeze.

'Thank you,' said William through a smile and while tipping his head slightly in gesture. In all his thirty years, he could never recall a time where he had forgotten his manners; his late mother made sure of that.

You could tell that the woman had beauty in her youth from her soft features: a pale blonde bob neatly framed a face that would look naked if not for the dainty glasses she wore. Although she had aged well for a lady of seventy, her skin was touched by wrinkles and each line told its own tale. A gold rope necklace coupled with a Christ companion chain dangled around her collar and three gilded rings marked their territory on her wedding finger, one of which grabbed William's attention as being something quite remarkable.

The gold ring had an elegant pattern carved in its loop and in the middle was held a round diamond that sparkled in every imaginable colour. The owner had caught William staring at her ring, but wasn't at all inclined to offer any commentary on it. It was obvious that each piece of jewellery had not been touched for years from the way the slack skin had formed around them.

As William sat beside this woman, trying to think of the most natural way to strike up a conversation, it occurred to him that somehow, she had found a more rewarding vantage point of the park than he had. William's stomach sickened slightly at the thought of the few years he had wasted viewing a slice of the world from a single standpoint without ever considering the possibility that there might be a superior perspective. From his new spot, William could see the sunset in all its glory; the way its magnificent orange glow caressed the horizon before sulking into the darkness.

He could have said something to her, anything even, but William thought it more fitting, in that particular moment, to say nothing at all. Just being there next to her and filling that void carried certain poignancy - after all, William was afraid that if he had spoken, he might just have made things worse for the old girl who was so used to having her husband beside her.

If she wanted to talk, she would, William thought. But she never did.

Day followed day, and night followed night, until William felt he knew all about the woman, yet they never exchanged a single sentence in conversation - just smiles.

As the summer days edged closer to autumn, William noticed her hands tucked deeper into her pockets and her scarf wrapped tighter around her neck. William observed that she was a woman who was easily buffeted by the breeze, however slight. On occasion, he would offer her his own scarf and once his hat in jest, neither of which she accepted, of course - instead mutely declining, but with appreciation.

On this particular day, William took to the park bench a little later than usual but still in plenty of time for the sunset.

As always, the woman was already there and waiting, but not for him – instead, for something else - something that made William think that perhaps he should be waiting for it, too. He had no idea what, though. Just that it was something good, judging by the sneaky smile that the woman held across her face and her keen eyes, as they dizzied inside of her head.

William gazed out over the landscape, looking at what the day had to offer in the way of beauty, but it was hard to ignore the burning lamp in the sky; it hogged his peripheral and demanded as much attention as a smudge on a clear canvas.

Suddenly, William's gaze was stolen away by a young woman approaching at the foot of the hills and coming up past the spot where he had once sat. In that moment, he had forgotten all about the sun in its descent and was completely immersed in a different kind of beauty. Everything around her was little more than a blur. She had the most exquisite hair: long, wavy and golden to threaten the sun. She looked no more than twenty-eight years of age and William could tell she was a lady, a woman of class judging by her elegant gait and the way she dressed. The elderly companion beside him suddenly perked up as if what she had been waiting for on this very day had finally arrived.

William knew, despite his sweating palms and the lump that had recently formed in his throat, that he had to introduce himself to her. He found himself devising a ridiculous plan of approach, which amounted to nothing more than a jolting reminder of his own incompetence in gender relations. Nonetheless, he wasn't about to let that stop him from at least trying, for William knew only too well that if he hadn't, he would live to regret it.

William sat struggling to think of something to say to the young woman, should he find the courage to even approach her.

The sound of silence was so marked that he could hear the words fumbling around in his mind, bickering needlessly amongst themselves.

'That was me fifty years ago. And you're my husband,' said the widow to William and without adjusting her gaze from where it landed upon the young lady.

Startled, William came out from his reverie and slowly twisted a look towards her.

After days, weeks even, of comfortable silence and wondering, William finally heard what this woman's voice sounded like and it was exactly as he imagined it to be: gentle, quietly soothing and full of love; there was even something strangely familiar about it.

Given that she was looking towards the same splendour that had so soon stolen his heart, he had some idea of what she was talking about but wasn't entirely sure as to what she wanted him to say in return. William didn't like to engage in conversation from fear of letting this beautiful girl slip away, but at the same time, he had no intention of being ill-mannered and snubbing the chance of conversing with the dear woman who he had spent his recent weeks sat beside.

Yet again, William's eyes revealed his mind at work, as he contemplated his next move and spent far too long doing it. He sat stroking his lower lip, scrambling through his plethora of words, looking for those fit for speech.

'What are you still doing here?' said the lady, and for a moment, authority commandeered the gentleness in her voice. 'If my husband had just sat here as I walked through this park, I never would have met the love of my life. Now get up and go meet yours.'

It had all become apparent to William. Why this lady visited the park each day, why she always sat in the same spot, looked over the same hill and why she chose that precise moment to speak to him.

She came into William's life as a shade of Cupid, seeking to spark a new romance that was faithful to her own. It was rather abundant to her that William hadn't already a lover in his life for he wouldn't be spending his days sat beside an aged woman if he had.

Again, William resorted to niceties and extended a kind, genuine thank you to the gentle being who had changed his life forever.

William took his leave and mimicked the gleaming smile that smacked itself upon the woman's face. She was happy to see William about to relive her fondest memory; it was almost as if her own journey had reached the end of its loop and was about to be reborn.

Although no tangible sentence formed in his mind, only random words in random orders, it didn't matter because he felt good.

He set the sweet young lady in his sights and began to walk, half hesitant, half determined.

William paused in his stride to glance back at the bench and as he did so, he noticed that the eyes of his bench companion were firmly fixed upon him. As he edged closer to the young woman - who was now stood alone by an ice cream counter, which was still, so late in the afternoon, swarming with children like bees to a hive - he felt the gaze burn a hole in his back.

His knees weakened and William suddenly felt the uncertainty of the soft ground beneath his feet, yet it mattered not, because every step took him closer to where he so desperately wanted to be.

William had no idea what he was going to say or how it was all going to turn out, but there was something undeniably exhilarating about the uncertainty of it all. For some strange reason, that walk across the park felt like a lifetime; his world had slowed down, yet he was moving so fast.

At last, he arrived at the feet of the most beautiful thing he had ever seen. She looked up at him with these bright blue eyes that stared out of an angelic face sprinkled with the palest of freckles.

The thief had returned to steal his breath, but it was too important to let him take it this time. He squeezed the words from his mouth, peppering them with as much charm as he could muster under the pressure, all the while being too conscious of trying not to choke on them.

'That lady, up there on the bench, she said I should come and introduce myself to the love of my life. I can only assume she meant you?' said William in the most unrehearsed fashion and while anxiously stroking a hand through his dark hair.

CHAPTER TWO

Lily Jayne

Although the day was slipping into night, the fine clear weather held long enough for all that William had planned.

He gestured to the elderly woman who was sat watching their encounter with as much excitement as a child on Christmas Eve, and although Lily tracked his gaze, she threw surprisingly little attention to it.

'How do you know she meant me? There are other women around here,' she said, mesmerising William with her cute lilt while surveying her surroundings and noticing the other busying ladies.

William observed that, although she was stunning to the eye, the girl acted innocent, as if she didn't know it, and he liked that about her.

'But none as hypnotic as you,' replied William, completely unaware of the words that he was speaking.

Lily blushed and smiled at the same time.

William had surprised himself at how adept he was at swooning the lady after all. Her cheeks shone a bright pink to match the colour of her lips while the soft furrows in her face formed around a picture-perfect smile.

'Is this how you speak to all the women in your life?' asked Lily, with cheeky intent. 'Using an old lady to rope them in?'

William didn't see that coming, but he could sense why she may have surmised that.

What could I say that she would believe? William pondered, while trying his utmost not to appear awkward in the meantime; something that never came too easy.

'It is true. I confess,' said William, as he raised a hand in submission. 'I like to carry an elderly lady with me wherever I go because I just never know when I'm going to need one.'

To William's relief, Lily immediately found the hilarity in his sarcasm and raised her smile even wider.

'No,' continued William, evenly. 'She merely gave me the nudge I needed to come over here.'

'Well, I'm sure she's glad that you did,' said Lily, while slipping off her white fabric gloves.

'Yes. But are you?' asked William, seeking to gauge her reaction in which he expected to find reassurance that he was, in fact, out of her league.

'We'll have to see about that one, won't we?' After a slight pause, the girl spoke, but with a tinge of cheekiness that suggested to William that they would get along just fine together.

Although it was a more promising response than William had hoped for, he could already start to feel the conversation falling flat. He didn't expect his encounter to last quite as long as it did, let alone prepare for it. In fact, he bore such little confidence in himself that he thought he would be returning to the bench before his seat grew cold.

There was so much to talk about, yet no words were being spoken. *How am I to rescue the conversation, or, at least, buy myself some time?* William thought, while Lily was waiting for him to say something…anything.

'My name is Lily.' Filling the void, she hung her hand gently in the air between them, inviting William to take it and to take her.

'Lily. That's a beautiful name,' replied William, as he raised her hand to his lips and planted a soft kiss upon it.

Lily stood waiting to hear William speak his name, but he moved past the moment, swiftly, and for no particular reason.

'May I have the pleasure of buying the lady an ice cream?' said William, surprised at how he had managed to get so far with her and believing this to be where it must all fall apart.

What am I saying? She's not five years old, why would she want me to buy her an ice cream?

William froze for a moment just to allow his consciousness to get the best of him.

'Sure,' said Lily with a childish giggle. 'Thank you.'

While Lily browsed the selection of flavours on offer that day, William used the brief moment of excusable nothingness to store conversation starters in his head for when the time came again to speak.

William guided Lily towards a hilltop where they sat together. They talked, they laughed and they gave an avid audience to the sunset.

As they relaxed into the company of one another, it began to feel natural and William had departed with the overwhelming sense of panic that had previously governed his thoughts.

In the midst of his delight, William twisted a look behind him to find that the lady had taken her leave from the bench. It was the first time that she had removed herself from the green ahead of William, and, much to his displeasure, he was never to see the elderly woman there again.

The couple remained on the hilltop until there was no light left save that of the stars. William rested flat on the cold grass and he could feel the weight of his own body as it sunk into the ground. He coupled his hands and tucked them behind his head to provide a small degree of comfort against the hardness of the land. William heard the hooting of owls and the loons calling out from their watery bed; it was like a melody was being composed in the near darkness to an underscore of gentle wind and crickets. As he gave himself to nature's rhythm, Lily wrapped her cardigan tight around her shoulders and planted her head lightly on his chest.

William smiled to himself before curling his arm around Lily's shoulder, pulling her in closer.

'This is nice,' Lily whispered. William understood why she had whispered, for the place was so peaceful, like another world even.

Together they looked at the stars and whoever was returning their gaze was looking down at a picture perfect postcard.

William moved his fingers upward, gently stroking them through her hair.

'Yes,' he put in.

CHAPTER THREE

Locked in Love

31 JULY, 1909. NEARLY ONE YEAR LATER.

The evening was exceptionally warm and the air stuck to the lovers like glue. The strange noises of the night perturbed their silence, but it made them feel alive, watched by nature and protected by it.

'I love you,' William whispered, as the night began to grow dark around them. He had never said that before, but he so often felt it.

Although she returned the sentiment, the single second it took for Lily to answer seemed like a decade. William was so gloriously in love with her that it made his skin prickle to think that she may not feel the same way; but she did, and he knew that.

'Forever,' added the girl whose heart had been broken once already.

Despite William's awkwardness on the subject, Lily told him all about her previous lover, the way he controlled her and often scared her. She found something cathartic in sharing her painful experiences, but William found no such thing in the hearing of them. All he could do was listen and promise he would treat her better; treat her the way she deserved to be treated.

William whispered to her, but she never spoke back; it's funny how words get lost in the dark. With Lily quiet and drifting off to sleep, William made no further attempt at conversation, as he didn't like to risk drawing her from her slumber. Instead, he wrapped her in his arms and held her as if she was born to be held.

There was but little around in the way of furniture, as the bedroom was used primarily for sleeping. A four-poster bed was the core feature and it hogged most of the floor space. There was a chest of drawers and a standing wardrobe pushed up against the wall by the door, but the overpowering and majestic cradle demoted the rest of the objects to your peripheral. There was no lighting save that of a bedside gas lamp, gently illuminating William and Lily, while burning away at their silhouettes.

As they rested together, snug in the warmth of their bed and couched in each other's arms, a cool breeze cut unseen through the white velvet drapes like a shadow in the darkness. The air slithered through the grooves of their naked entangled bodies with a refreshing chill upon its breath.

William took a moment to smell Lily's magnificently wild hair; the golden locks that poised in front of him as if he were face down on a lion's back. Her perfumed aroma raced through every inch of him, replacing the sweaty odour that had not long since raided his nostrils. In that moment of stillness, all thoughts were pushed from his mind - all except that of their anniversary the next day.

They didn't say goodnight. They slowly drifted into a deep slumber, locked in love and tired from making it.

CHAPTER FOUR

The Strange Market Square

THE SAME NIGHT. THREE YEARS LATER.

Shortly before ten o'clock, the quietness of the air grew quite repressive and the silence was so marked that the howling of a hound in the village was distinctly heard – the echoing sound was like a discord in the vast harmony of nature's silence.

Through the noise, William and Lily made love like it was their last time; William embraced her like it would *be* the last time.

'I love you,' William whispered.

'Forever,' added the girl whose heart had been broken already.

His name was Eddy Heward. Despite William's awkwardness on the subject, Lily told him all about Eddy, the way he controlled her and often scared her. She found something cathartic in sharing her painful experiences but William found no such thing in the hearing of them. In fact, it brought him nothing but pain. All he could do was listen and promise he would treat her better; treat her the way she deserved to be treated.

William whispered to her, but she never spoke back; it's funny how words get lost in the dark.

The tired gas lamp fell asleep in agreement with the jaded lovers. In that sleep, William dreamt an old dream of Lily lying limp on a bed of blood whilst the cold darkness closed in around her. He moved in to kneel down beside her and as he did so, Lily awoke from her death to smile up at him. The same dream touched William in the dark every night, but he could never make sense of it.

*

The next morning had dawned cold and clear, with a freshness that suggested a premature end to summer.

William awoke to the sound of hooves trotting by the open window and the village butcher attracting local custom in the most traditional fashion.

William gently retracted his numb arm from beneath the angel that slept beside him, cautious not to disturb her. She was always a heavy sleeper, but you wouldn't know it. Her cheeks softened around lips that were only lightly pressed together. Her eyelids would sometimes twitch, which made William think that she was only on the brink of sleep and that a pin drop could wake her. There was nothing hard about her features that suggested in any way that she was in a deep slumber.

Despite his tendency to, William didn't watch her for too long because if anything could draw Lily from her sleep, it was his musky morning breath by which he was so often embarrassed.

As it was their yearly anniversary, William had plans to prepare them both a romantic candlelit supper.

He silently slipped away and proceeded to dress in his best clothing that suitably marked the occasion. He wore dark tailored trousers, a pale striped shirt that he used only during the day and a high-buttoned, single-breasted waistcoat with a cutaway morning jacket to defend against the fresh breeze. Upon leaving the apartment, William swiped his bowler hat from the rack by the door and in the same motion placed it upon his head, completing his smart daytime attire.

*

The misty breath of man and mount mingled in Mane's Market Square, a hub thriving with trade and that stood proudly at the heart of the village and just a short walk across the cobbled streets from William's apartment.

The clock tower waited for William to arrive at the market before striking nine bells. The sound rang loud and true, drowning out the many noises of people going about their morning. The Square was busy with friendly faces and interactions, but no more or less so than a typical Saturday morning.

Stood quietly, and rather shadily, too, behind a vegetable wagon was the lonely Mr Busk, wrapped up like an Eskimo in a blizzard. *Sure, the air was fresh but it wasn't that cold.* William had always joked with Mr Busk about how he had often felt the cold even in the height of summer. Lately, though, William had got the impression that he may have made one joke too many, for the man's demeanour was unusually sultry in his presence.

Mr Busk isn't exactly a fast mover, but he always did well to avoid William when nearby. Just last week, they accidentally collided around a blind spot near Mrs Collins's Candy Counter, causing Mr Busk to let loose of his shopping bags.

'I beg your pardon, Mr Busk. Please, let me get those for you,' said William in a neighbourly fashion despite the man's blatantly ignorant disposition.

William had knelt down to gather the man's items, but when he stood back up, Mr Busk had vanished; he had just abandoned his groceries. William looked around him, but the gentleman was nowhere to be seen.

It had crossed his mind that he disappeared to avoid conversation, which William thought was rather odd, but believable given Mr Busk's evasive behaviour of late. William thought that the man, as lonely as he always appeared, would appreciate a little neighbourly interaction, but sometimes people get set in their ways, however peculiar they may seem to the outside world, and William respected that.

As he waded through the market, William felt passing eyes turn away as if he had something hideous plastered on his forehead; he paid little attention to it though, as sadly he had grown used to it.

With renewed purpose, William located the butcher's holler and made short work of getting there.

'Conway, just the man,' said William, as he threw a pointed finger playfully towards him upon arrival.

The man was big and round, with not a single hair upon his head. His flesh was a vibrant pink colour as if swollen with blood and he had the chunkiest of fingers that rather reminded William of the sausages that the man sold.

'How's business on this fine morning?' William spoke to him like an old friend, casual and offbeat.

'Why, 'ello there, William,' said the butcher while bagging a chunk of beef for a young woman there with her baby. 'Trade's good, y'know, but it could be better.' His country accent boomed and penetrated the market's busy atmosphere.

'I guess it could always be better, hey?' said William, as Conway was finishing up with the customer.

No matter what the day turned out, he had always received an enthusiastic welcome from the man, but this time, it felt a little more laid on than usual. He was rather quick to the chase, too.

'Two slabs of my prime steak *again* is it, sir?' said the butcher, stealing a glance at the clock tower and noting the time.

'Please,' said William, passing over the butcher's brevity. 'Tonight's a rather special evening.'

'Indeed it is.'

William dangled the thread of conversation, hoping that Conway would entreat him to share the details of his anniversary. Instead, the butcher threw down the steak, took the money and, before William could spark any further conversation or even put in a thank you, turned away rather abruptly and began serving his next customer, who was in no way ready to be received.

'Yes, madam, how can I help you?'

William took that as his invitation to continue about his business; he thought it best anyway as he was yet to bag the rest of his groceries and he didn't like the thought of Lily waking to an empty apartment.

CHAPTER FIVE

A Letter for Lily

Not an hour had passed before William was making his way back through the market bound for his apartment while staring at the strangeness about him.

From the moment William was born through to the ripe old age of thirteen, Mane proved itself to be an unruly beast. But then it flowered - its people, its businesses, everything, came to fruition and the air felt light, free of melancholy. Recent years, however, have seen the place return to old habits. Habits that saw Mane morph into a different kind of beast. *Since when did this place become so...odd?*

Although rife with sickness and poverty for a time, Mane was the only place that William had ever known and, as he sauntered home, he found a strange comfort in remembering the earlier years he had spent there.

William's memory spanned back over twenty years and if he closed his eyes, he could still smell the scarcity that spilled from the sooty tenement streets of his boyhood. He could taste on his lips the soggy bread that his mother served up for his supper.

In his heart, he felt his parents' misery as they tried to keep their family warm, safe and healthy in the place they called home.

Common disease controlled the neighbourhood and snuffed out life like a frosty breath on a warm candle's flame.

As he walked past one of the older houses in the town, William remembered hearing, while he played as a child on his front step, the tortured cries that floated from a nearby window. They were the screams of a woman dying from tuberculosis - a woman who couldn't afford any drugs to ease her departure from this mortal coil.

As he arrived outside his own boyhood home, the memory of the woman faded and another replaced it. It was one that bore far greater significance to William, and brought far greater pain, too; a pain that was to change him; define him.

It was the foul memory of diphtheria torturing his younger sister. William couldn't un-see his dear sibling wasting away before his eyes, and the shadows of the memories that he tried so desperately to forget plagued the rest of his childhood. It scarred him but left the outside untouched.

William remembered the morning she died. She was just ten years old and William had never felt such pain in all his life.

The family had no wealth to bury little Grace, so like the rest of the country's indigent, she was tipped anonymous into a pulpous pit. She died unnecessarily and far too early in a shameful era of austerity. Grace's death marked a barbarous time. A bleak time. A time that William prayed never to return to his doorstep.

The loss changed the family. Some were broken by it, others hardened. William's mother Rose blamed the neighbouring cities, as they would often move disease-ridden patients into quieter environments like Mane, isolated from industrial life and where the air was pure and freely circulating, only to prevent its spread and protect its own industries. Rose was appalled at how her village had become a dumping ground for the sick in a time when hospitals, doctors and medicine were but for the privileged few.

It was a sad thing that when William looked upon his childhood home, it stirred a pain that burrowed deep inside of him.

There were happier memories, too, of course: memories of his parents' undying love for him and of the few years growing up alongside his sister; the memories, too, of the friends that he grew up with and often played with in the streets outside of his house, and, if he listened closely, he could still hear the echoes of boyish laughter. But, for

William, happy memories were made redundant with such unhappy endings.

Nonetheless, it was those memories that made the place so special and which gave William and his family no cause to ever step beyond the boundaries of their village.

The cities that crowded Mane, those were the economic cities, the cities that robbed workingmen of their individuality, booming with new industries and where mechanisation was increasing the number of unskilled workers.

William's father Ralph, however, had escaped the debilitating factory labour. He was a craftsman, quite talented with his hands, although not much good at anything else. He was a master shoemaker by trade, but after the death of his daughter, he picked up extra work as a bootblack and from repairing bicycles out of a wooden shack in his back yard where villagers would deliver their custom.

Ralph needed to keep his mind constantly occupied else he would plummet into a pit of despair. William admired his father for recognising that and for finding the strength to continue providing for his family.

Rose was alright, she was a tough girl; in losing Grace, she learned to love William even more. She loved him tirelessly to the point where Ralph feared she'd suffocate him. Rose wasn't to blame, though. The injustice of losing her little sweetheart galvanised her emotions and hardened her into a rock; hardened more so by the fear of outliving another child.

Rose grew up in Mane and as a young woman worked as a domestic servant to Lord Botham. She became a teacher at Mane Primary School after she met and married Ralph. That was until Rose entered motherhood and was forced to give it up for a while to see her children to an age where she may return to the work that she so enjoyed.

As William continued to walk through the streets of Mane with his mind racing down the avenues of his bygone years, he felt as if he was being taken on a journey, guided by the streets themselves. William knew that beyond the church was the graveyard and in the graveyard, laid the parents that he missed every day.

Ralph died a sudden death when William had approached his twenties. He had lived a largely healthy lifestyle and the cause of his death was unclear, but again, Rose accused the industries.

As William had dedicated his time at school to becoming a writer and was experimenting with poetry at the time of his father's death at the age of fifty-seven, Rose sold her husband's businesses and assets so that she and William may continue to live in the way that they had become accustomed to.

However, it wasn't long after Ralph's death that Rose, having marginally survived childbirth, gave her life to influenza, leaving William to inherit the little wealth that the family had left; which was mainly spent on laying to rest his mother for whom he had cared so deeply. Rose was the family's pillar of strength and William liked to lean.

Within a space of a few short years, the boy had lost all that remained of his family. He felt an enormous gap in his life, a gap large enough to eat him alive; William sometimes felt so depressed that he considered letting it take him, chew him through and through and swallow him down its little red lane until he felt nothing.

There was a stubborn void that he could never manage to fill, and no matter how much he burdened the paper with his thoughts, no matter how many poems he gave readings to, there was always this emotional vacancy. That was until Lily walked into his life. The moment he set his eyes on her was the moment he felt half whole again.

As William reminisced over the day he and Lily encountered, he was suddenly coloured with a childish excitement by their anniversary.

While the thoughts of both his parents and his lover battled for prominence in his active recollecting, William walked the final stretch of narrow windswept streets that were carpeted in cobblestone before arriving at the door to his apartment.

The door was small, innate and pressed up against Caine's Chemist, above which was his bedsit.

As a way of paying the rent, William had worked at the chemist for a time when he had first taken lodgings there, but he soon grew too engulfed in his writing to help Mr

Caine out. Besides, the shop doesn't seem to see much trade anymore, not since the old man had his accident; knocked over right outside he was, by a horse pulling a carriage. It was unnatural the way this particular horse was being whipped that it was no wonder the beast lost its nerve. Poor Mr Caine was just in the wrong place at the wrong time, with his hands too full of medicines to stand a chance of breaking his fall and preventing his injuries; the irony of it all was rather striking.

*

As William stepped through the doorway, he collected the mail that had since gathered in his absence. He then distributed the weight of the bags evenly across both hands so that he was suitably balanced, as he proceeded up the stairway and into his apartment.

William's corner plot was lavishly furnished compared to most of the neighbouring terraces. If you entered from the stairway to the left of the house, you found yourself stood in the living space, which was all open plan and although not at all spacious, it was larger than one might think from simply looking up from the outside.

Immediately to the left was the kitchen, which led through into the scullery and beyond that, an alcove sink that was used to wash both plates and bodies. Pushed up against the window in the kitchen, which looked out over the distant hills behind the building, was a white wood table that was built by one of the local carpenters some years ago. Lots of things were made of plain unvarnished white wood: the bread bin, the knife box, the plate-drainer and even the chopping board, as it leant the kitchen a clean and crisp ambience. The scullery had a side door that led down some steps and to the outside lavatory.

Next to the kitchen was the only bedroom and the wall that faced the front of the building was plotted with two windows framed by velvet drapes. Beneath the far window was a single armchair crowded by a mini table, upon which sat a gas lamp. At the foot of the window closest to the door was an ornate settee, clothed in patterned burgundy upholstery that upstaged its wooden frame. Slipped in next to the settee was William's writing desk that his parents had bought him for his eighteenth birthday, above which was a photograph of his parents, unsmiling but looking happy.

Squeezed between the two vertical windows was an open fireplace and on one side was a recess with a built-in cupboard in which was kept the crockery and food, except for the perishables, of course. A large rug, warm in colour, gave hiding to wooden flooring and on the ceiling dangled a gas mantle.

To William's frustration, Lily had awoken in his absence and moved to the couch, where she sprawled in her nightgown.

'Good morning, my dear.' Despite his annoyance, William was happy to see her, especially after the oddities he faced with the villagers in the market.

Lily didn't respond. She was already occupied, reading from what looked to William a lot like the parchment on which he would scribe his poetry.

'What is it you're reading there?' said William, oddly concerned over what she had found.

'Nothing,' she replied, with a suspicious inflection.

Lily wasn't allowed to read William's writings except for on the odd occasions when he would ask for her opinion. William was often quite precious with his work and he was saving his latest and most important limerick for that evening, where he had plans to read it to her over their low-lit anniversary celebrations.

William laid down his shopping and dashed over to Lily to discover she was reading an old piece - his ode to nature.

Somewhat relieved that she hadn't found the poem that he was deliberately keeping from her, he allowed himself to joke about her looking through his work.

William threw the letters that were still in the clutches of his hand down beside Lily and began playfully tickling her. She was extremely susceptible to his touch and she creased over in hysterics, rolling about the settee to the ebb and flow of his kind torture.

'Stop! Stop! Look, you're creasing the letters,' squealed Lily through her frenzied laughter.

William broke his tickling and collected the letters that had since packed themselves beneath Lily's leg.

'There's a letter for you,' said William, as he offered it to her.

'That's odd,' Lily replied, while her face demonstrated her curiosity. 'I never get post here.'

Lily took a moment to study the envelope and the return address on the rear of the packet served in aiding in her inquisitiveness.

'It's from Gran. Of course it is. She's the only one who would write me here.'

'Your gran?' said William, rather indifferently whilst studying his own post.

Lily's eyes ran down the page as she read the memo to herself.

'Yes...but it's not good news.' Lily's mood soured all of a sudden.

'What does it read?' From Lily's sullen tone, William felt he should pay a little more attention. He dropped his own correspondents and shuffled closer to Lily. 'May I?' He prized the note from her weak grasp and read it to himself, noticing that part of it, the upper corner, had been torn:

My dearest Lily,

I pray life in Mane is treating you well.

It is with regret that I write to you bearing bad news. I have fallen sick and I fear I haven't long left to live. I would like to see you soon and you are welcome to bring someone with you, a friend perhaps? I would feel better knowing you will be safe on your travels.

I had hoped that this letter would find you under better circumstances, but it is important that you know.

Please do not be too troubled by my news. I look forward to your visit.

All my love,
Gran.

P.S. I'm sure Abby will be happy to see you, too.

'I'm sorry to hear that, my love.' William embraced Lily, who had since began to weep, and after a short while, although somewhat inappropriate given the gravity of the situation, he questioned whether Lily's grandmother had any knowledge of him at all.

'You haven't told her about me yet, have you?'

For a moment, a silence separated their exchange of words.

'No,' Lily whispered while touched upon his shoulder.

'Are you embarrassed by me or something?'

'No! Of course I'm not,' said Lily, as she brusquely peeled away from William. 'She's just protective over me since...since Eddy.' She continued, while drying her eyes. 'So much so that she sent me away...sent me here. She doesn't trust any man, especially with me. Not after what happened.'

William began to feel sorry about ever approaching the subject, for he could see how torn up she was.

'So, I never told her. But it doesn't matter now, does it?' continued Lily, as she planted her hands back upon William. 'We can go visit her together and she can see you for herself. See that you're not a bad man like all the others.'

'And who's Abby?'

'She's just a childhood companion. I'll introduce you to her, too.' Lily drew closer to William and almost helped herself to a one-sided embrace.

'No. I think you should go by yourself?' said William, as he freed himself of Lily's limp hold. William's attitude was strikingly out of character, but it was born from his genuine upset. Lily keeping him a secret from her gran, and for so long, too, made William feel as if he wasn't good enough for her. He always held, in the back of his mind, the notion that he was out of her league and it was little things like this that reminded him of it.

'What? You'll let me go by myself?' Lily looked at William, curious and through eyes that looked as if they were not yet done leaking. 'But why?'

William hated seeing Lily saddened, but he didn't feel too good about accompanying her on her travels either. Putting aside his upset, he was bent on it being the wrong time to introduce himself to Lily's unsuspecting, and probably volatile, grandmother judging by what he had heard thus far.

'I wouldn't feel comfortable infringing on such a delicate matter,' said William as he began collecting the letters and clearing up the mess that they had made. 'It is a matter concerning family and it should remain so.'

For a time, Lily was lost for words. It was William's sudden coldness that rendered her temporarily speechless.

'Besides, she doesn't even know about me and if she is as ill as she says, then it is best that she doesn't get any last-minute surprises,' continued William as if he had some time to think of such a considered response.

'But I want you there. I need you there. Does that count for nothing?' Lily pleaded, but deep down, William knew that she shouldn't have to.

'I'm sorry,' said William, turning his attention now to the shopping bags. He had hoped to end the conversation there and for Lily to understand, but unfortunately for him, that wasn't the case.

'Do you not want to see where I grew up?' said Lily. 'I can take you to visit all my favourite childhood places.' She peppered her words with forced excitement and raised her mood in a last attempt to sway William's stubborn reasoning.

'Yes, it'll be fun,' said William, whilst pretending to busy himself with emptying the contents of the carrier bags. 'Afterwards, we can take a ride on your favourite swing and you can introduce me to your ex-lover. How does that sound?' He returned a powerful gaze to Lily only to be met with a cold one in return.

Again, Lily received yet another demonstration of William's sledgehammer sarcasm but not the type that had once brought a smile to her face.

Instead, William's attitude was sour, cutting through the tense and emotional atmosphere and twisting it in a different, much darker direction.

'You know something? Maybe you're not the man I thought you were. I can't believe you would even do this to me. I thought you were different. Such a fool I've been to think that there are some good men out there,' said Lily, coming to realise that perhaps her gran was right. 'Now, if you will excuse me, I should go pack. I've got a long journey ahead of me.' She threw the letter on the floor in a warranted huff and made across the living room to the bedroom.

William stopped toying with the ingredients of his evening meal.

'Wait. You're going tonight?' he said, with a blank expression.

'You read what Gran wrote,' replied Lily, as she turned to face him. 'She doesn't know how long she has left, so why would I hang around?'

'Look, Lily, I'm sorry.' William stepped up to Lily and took her softly by the hands. 'Listen, I had a special evening planned for us tonight. Don't go. Stay here with me and leave early in the morning. What do you say?'

'You don't understand, do you?' said Lily, as she ripped her hands from William's touch. 'It might not be important to you, but it's important to me. The special evening can wait until I return. Come with me or I leave without you?' Lily made one final bid to acquire his support, as she so desperately didn't want to travel alone.

'You're right, I don't understand. What's one more night?' said William in a selfish frenzy.

'One night could be the difference between seeing my gran once more and never getting the chance to say goodbye,' said Lily, as her eyes glazed over. 'I didn't have parents growing up. Gran was all I had and now she...'

William could see the tremor in her lips as she was about to cry, but for some reason resisted the compulsion to comfort her.

'You know, I don't need to explain this to you,' continued Lily, managing to resist the natural urge to wet her face with tears. 'If you're too self-absorbed to realise how important this is to me, then maybe you shouldn't come.'

'Fine by me.' William could see the repulsive way in which he was treating his beloved sweetheart, yet he could do nothing to help himself. It was as if he was merely a voyeur, peering in on a darker shade of himself, absent of influence.

'You're unbelievable, William,' shouted Lily, as she continued into the bedroom while finally breaking out into tears.

Lily began packing her belongings in an audibly emphasised fashion. Not knowing how long she'd be gone, Lily packed a little more than she perhaps needed and quickly, too, as she cringed at being in William's company any longer than she had to. It wasn't that she hated him, or even fallen out of love with him, just that she couldn't stand the sight of him in that moment.

Lily slammed shut the bedroom door as she made for the exit, with the harsh and painful words, 'Don't expect me back' in place of a passionate goodbye.

William let her go and didn't say a word. He wished he could speak, plead for her to stay, to forgive him already, but he was numb. He just sat on the couch rethinking his behaviour and quickly coming to regret acting in the most brutish and unforgivable way.

CHAPTER SIX

Left Behind Again

Although William had lived alone before, everything felt strange without Lily. In her absence, the only place he could find a reasonable degree of relief from the gut-wrenching pain of solitude was sat at his writing desk, scribing his thoughts before attempting to mould them into either letters to Lily or works of respectable literature.

Day after day he would spend hours just sat at his desk with his pen companion crafting sentence after sentence, thinking about its structure and its rhythm and if he fell short of inspiration, which he often did, he would find it in a photograph he kept of his parents.

The frame proudly occupied a prominent position upon William's desk. His mother and father were stood, holding hands and, although unsmiling, they looked happy.

The days were tough but bearable. It was the nights that troubled him the most; all the times that he spent just laying awake in bed, gazing at nothing and feeling detached from everything and everyone.

Each night, after his stream of consciousness burnt itself out and when he eventually shutdown into sleep, he dreamt an old dream of Lily lying limp on a bed of blood while the cold darkness closed in around her. William moved in to kneel down beside her and as he did so, Lily awoke from her death to smile up at him.

The same dream touched William in the dark every night, but he could never make sense of it. Sometimes he would be so afraid of having the same dream that he would remain at his desk all night; but somehow it still found him.

Stung by guilt's tail, William was held in hurt's wake and felt numb from head to toe.

As he sat alone by the fire, he was reminded of the vacancies that his lover drew there. He felt trapped in the space between happiness and hardness, free of her presence and laughter.

William eventually detached himself from his self-pity and twisted a gaze out the window.

Amidst the darkened plume were tiny lights that shone brightly. *Under the same set of stars, we lay worlds apart* was William's lasting thought as the bloody dream came in with an army to take him.

CHAPTER SEVEN

He's Coming

The first letter William had waited a week before sending. He knew that Lily would have better things to do than to read him grovel and pine for her.

The weeks rolled by as slow as a snail slithering backwards on a razor's edge, each day leaving a thicker trail of slime in his mind and obscuring his thoughts.

One letter after the next, he sent his moods and affections on parchment to the return address exactly as it appeared on Gran's letter to Lily:

RIDDLE MANOR
WEEPERS HOLLOW
ENGLAND

Twenty-eight days had passed since Lily had left him cold and alone, and in those twenty-eight days not one letter had William received in response to his many. It was hard to think that Lily was simply ignoring him, but it was harder to think that something might have happened to her.

William had decided to send one last letter, but this one was to inform Lily of his journey to the country and to her:

28 AUGUST, 1912

Lily,

...I will be journeying to Weepers Hollow on Friday, 30 August, taking the four minutes past ten train from Mane, travelling around the Marsh Land via Deadman's Cross and up through Holmwood Forrest. I expect it will take me a few days, a little longer perhaps, as I am unversed in travel and all I have is the address to find you. But I will find you, and I eagerly wait the day that I am to hold you once more.

Until I see you again, my love x

CHAPTER EIGHT

The Journey East

William was nervous at the prospect of leaving Mane for the first time in his life, yet the whole thing felt rather familiar. As his father had once said, "The good in travelling was that it represented an escape from the local particular," and for William, nothing was more calculated to raise his spirits than the sight of his loved one, running into his arms and glowing like a freshly forged sword.

Motivated as he was, William set out to pack his things. He wondered how that would delay him, as he had no idea of what he should take or for how long he was to be away. To his surprise, the process of gathering his luggage was swift and soon, William was ready to set off on his journey east, dubious, but glad to be leaving his lodgings behind.

Out the door he felt the touch of morning, the burning of the frost and the good friends that he had lost. William tried to remember the faces that once greeted his doorstep, but they had become distant. The years leeched at his memories, not just of his friends who had all turned their backs and since faded into obscurity, but of those he vowed never to forget.

The empty streets felt more desolate than usual. It was often a quiet place, at least on non-market days, but William had witnessed, firsthand, the village morphing into a ghost town of sorts; it was as if Mane had sold its soul to the devil for safe passage into the underworld.

With his small brown suitcase in hand, William trekked through the village that was no longer his friend. He trekked down the lanes that would twist and turn and he trekked past the eyes that would single him out and burn.

It didn't take William long to reach the station as Mane was a small place. The single platform that carried passengers both to and from this once polite holding stretched out its paving behind the bell tower that stood high and mighty over the Market Square.

He knew the train would be arriving at the station at four minutes past ten and he gave himself just enough time to get there at a leisurely pace.

As he stood waiting in the wind's way, he heard the bellow of the steam engine approaching from a view obstructed by the church and its ignorant spire.

He focused his hearing like a whale in the deep and his ears captured all sorts of sounds: the chug of the rods, the hissing of the steam, the trumpet of the pistons, the screeching of the breaks and the attendant's whistle that was used to mark both the stop and start of motion.

William took each sound as layers to an internal rhythm and he was moved by it. At last, he found something beautiful again. He already felt as if he was transported, yet he stood still where the train had met him.

On approach, the train introduced itself as the Lanky Locomotive. It was a good-looking machine, not at all lanky but instead quite neat and proportioned as far as a hunk of metal goes.

A fellow passenger disembarking the train and brushing by him at an unnecessarily close distance detached William from his internal orchestra just in time for him to make the final boarding call. He confidently embarked the locomotive as if he had been on plenty of them before.

He took to the first empty compartment and was already impressed by the level of comfort it had guaranteed. The carriage had a cushioned couch laced in warm red velvet and was predictably soft to the touch. Matching red drapes were arranged neatly by the window and tied back in a way that honoured the daylight. The smell, although musty, made William feel comfortable as it awoke a fond memory in him.

It was the gentle recollection of Nanny June and of the smell that he had associated with her.

Filling the interior of her tiny house was always the full-bodied scent of old air. It wasn't sweet, but it wasn't bitter, either. It so often stuck to William's clothes, giving away the secret of his whereabouts and irritating those who couldn't stand the smell. The odour was an accumulation of everything inside of the house: the cooking, the fire, the dirt and grime brought in by William's grandfather and the dust that laid heavy in the carpets, furniture and curtains. It had always bore that same smell because June never liked to open any of the windows, not even whilst cleaning. She so often felt the cold and didn't like to suffer the draft, no matter how small. "Shut that door," she'd say, each time a door was opened or even just ajar, and in time, the air just grew stale.

William filled his lungs with the aroma that made his heart smile and cry at the same time. He took a second to muse on how a simple smell could take you back to a different time and place and just hold you there for as long as you let it.

Before settling down in the carriage, William hung his coat and hat on the hook by the door and he placed his luggage on the rack above the seat. He was to travel just over a day before changing at Deadman's Cross and he had braced himself for the long trek east.

To break the promised tedium, he had packed his literature with the intention of making headway on his next piece of writing. Although he had no idea what that next piece would be, he trusted his imagination to present him with it, for he found it rather counterproductive ever searching for inspiration.

In his professional activities, William carried a lesson with him that he learned while training in his craft. "Sometimes if you find yourself thinking too hard for a subject for a story or a limerick of some kind, then you're already condemning the writing process. Because you've forced that spark of imagination, you'll find it has no depth when it comes to fleshing it out. The spark has to be inspired to be worthwhile." In his clouded mind, William could hear Mrs King's words as clear as day. He never put pen to paper unless he felt that the spark was genuine, spontaneous and carried a niggling desire to have it's jugular sliced and to bleed out over the page.

William never chose his subjects, rather they came to him, and they would often come out of nowhere; sometimes it was in the middle of the night, sometimes in the middle of the day and would sometimes even stem from something as tiny and as quaint as a word spoken in a stranger's conversation. William would get incredibly obsessed that he just had to write about it and it pleased him to make something up rather than think about why he is who he is and to have to give birth to a story from his reality.

Beyond the glass, it was swiftly dark and, when the carriage curtains were pulled across, all was as snug and private as William's own lamplit study. William gave himself to the cosiness he felt as he drifted off to sleep, for come morning, he would need to make a change.

*

William changed at the busy station of Deadman's Cross with ease. He boarded his second train just past 08:00 and he had estimated that part of his trip to take half a day at most. He took notice as the track began to deviate north towards Holmwood Forrest, as well as bearing east.

It was shortly after the change that William began to feel uncomfortable, for the air was a great deal icier and was raging in draughts from the east with an unpleasant flood upon its breath.

The characteristics of the train in which he was to travel for the remainder of his journey paled considerably in comparison to the Lanky. William felt like a hostage, held in a comfortless carriage and forced to drop anchor on stiff pigskin. William ran a single finger down the window – that closer resembled a sheet of glass rattling in a timber frame - and the grime clung to his digit like iron to a magnet. The floors, wooden in texture, gave an unwilling surface to all sorts of muck. The state of the carriage was so repulsive that William had even considered tugging on the emergency chain.

For some while, William rolled on in the vile train, in silence - save that of the rain firing at will at his window and the tired huffing of the engine. William too had grown rather weary from travelling, methodically worn down by the sitting still and the bitter cold, as it found its way into his compartment and into his bones. He felt imprisoned in this cold tomb of a railway carriage and too far from any human dwelling for his own liking. He rubbed at the window and peered out to see nothing but the thick forest, asleep in the height of the afternoon, and William didn't think that a bad idea. Although it took some finding, William discovered his comfort and settled to sleep for the last few hours of his tedious trip.

After an arduous journey that spanned thirty-two long and relatively unproductive hours, the train pulled into Weepers Hollow Station just in time for William to witness the day slipping into night.

CHAPTER NINE

Weepers Hollow

The dark September night was still. A peculiar smell hung in the air - sour almost - kind of like what foreboding would smell like if such a thing ever did have an odour.

As the only passenger to disembark the train at his location, William found himself in a strangely familiar place, but without direction. The place rather reminded him of his hometown, not how it used to be, but rather the empty space it had become.

Weepers Hollow was little more than an imposter of a village, tucked away with its back turned on the world and with nothing to show in the way of attraction. It was no surprise that William was its only visitor that night.

As he stood there feeling about the sharp edges of his situation and staring into a weary place calling itself Weepers Hollow, the Hollow stared right back at him, but with a deadpan expression that made William shudder with intimidation.

The overwhelming sense of hostility he felt, as he stood alone and too aware of the fact, crawled under his skin like a scarab.

The narrowing streets were vacant but neighbourhood eyes spied from behind their closed drapes, smug as if they were invisible; and if William had his way, they *would* be.

William didn't know how to proceed or *where* in fact to proceed. He pulled his coat collar up, lowered the peak of his hat and began to walk in what looked to be the most promising direction.

Although he had no idea what to expect from the people outside of his own domain, William had rather hoped for a more comforting welcome on his first venture out of Mane. He could still see the station from where he stood, yet he already longed for home. With the memory of Lily's smile anchored in the forefront of his mind, he pushed on with purpose.

Weepers Hollow was a maze to a foreigner. William stumbled down countless passages, each one resembling that of the last and none showing any promise of progress.

William sauntered aimlessly for some time. His whole body stiffened around his core as he braced himself against the vulnerability he felt, which heightened each time at blind corners on approach. But the vulnerability he experienced was nothing but a weak thing when set against such strong will.

After his long journey, William didn't take too well to still being held in the bitter grasp of the outside. He so desperately sought warmth to defrost his bones, but the Hollow was not all that kind to him and the inbound weather showed no intention of allaying its mood.

As the night grew darker around him, William began to wonder how such a small place could present such a significant challenge. It had been over an hour already since he first set out stumbling about the place and yet not a single person had he encountered who might direct him to Riddle Manor and to his beloved Lily; it was as if the place had turned itself inside out and was hiding from him.

William thought that perhaps he could take shelter at the station until sunrise, if only he could trust himself to find his way back there. Instead, he continued the habit of the evening and walked further into a village shamefully uncluttered by signposts and people.

At last, in the near distance, there were lights from a building that William had somehow managed to miss. As he caught sight of the illuminated structure, his spirits rose and he began to feel rather more like a man of society than a wanderer of the underworld.

As he drew nearer, William viewed an ill-kept man exiting the building, evidently intoxicated from the way he was falling over nothing. The audible antics of the drunkard bludgeoned the silence in cold blood.

With a swift change of pace, William made haste for The Slaughters Barrel. The tavern stood alone, bent and top heavy with many windows dotted on the second floor. It occurred to William that perhaps there were bedrooms for rent above the drinker itself. The building looked as if it had been standing for many years and was now at the age where it was beginning to shrink and hunch over like Quasimodo. Dark passages, leading in almost every direction, cornered the Barrel and cut it off from the rest of the Hollow.

The weather had recently taken an unpleasant turn and had started with the wind growing ever harsher. With each step closer William took towards The Slaughters Barrel, the harder the wind blew as if trying to push him back; but all that did was make the promise of shelter even more appealing.

The inebriated gentleman by the entrance, although showed no guarantee of making any sense, presented William with his first opportunity to converse with a local in the hope of aiding him in his quest.

He was a great oaf of a man. A thick beard masked the majority of his face, naturally grey in colour but yellowed from a lifetime of smoke. He had the tiniest eyes that hid deep into his face and his hair was so wild, it was hard to tell where it ended and where his beard began. His clothes resembled that of a drifter, unclean and torn in places that William didn't like to look for too long.

'Excuse me, sir?' The man had most likely never been addressed as 'sir' in his entire life and although the place was rude to William, he was a guest and he didn't like to forget his manners.

William didn't know whether the man was hard of hearing or whether he was just too drunk to notice, but he was finding it rather difficult to be acknowledged.

'*Excuse me*, sir?!' The conviction in William's voice the second time around caused the man, whose own urine had recently spilled down his leg, to face him. However, to William's expected disappointment, there was no sense to be made of the blabbering that poured out of his mouth like the ample amounts of liquor that had not long since been poured in the opposite direction.

For a moment, William found himself locked in a one-way conversation, staring at the man's mouth and seeing it move, but not hearing anything that was coming out; only smelling the pungent pong of whisky that floated from his breath like steam from a kettle.

Having wasted so much of the day already, William left the man to entertain himself and advanced through into The Slaughters Barrel in the hope of procuring warmth, refreshment and most importantly, answers.

CHAPTER TEN

The Slaughters Barrel

The wind had either died down already or else could not be heard in the cover of the building.

Upon sight of the open fire, the discomfort that the day had presented William thus far melted away like his enthusiasm to be gone from Mane.

William's bones began to let loose their grip and he felt warm enough already to remove his coat and hat and to hang them on the rack, which stood just outside the door that leads through into the bar area, where he could, in fact, hear ample noise.

With a smile splashed upon his face and the promise of progress running true in his veins, William pushed through into the common area of the bar to discover that his presence was the trigger of an awkward silence. As William attempted to make eye contact with the people who had abruptly hushed, he noted that not a single set of eyes were held in his direction and wondered if anybody had even seen him arrive.

Upon entrance, William took a second to acquaint himself with the interior of the pub. To the left, one-half of an L-shaped bar ran parallel to a row of tables and benches that had a tired look about them as they peered out of a large window to the right. The other half of the bar extended around towards the rear and faced the drinkers who were partaking in a quiet game of darts. At the far end, just beyond the first row of benches, was an alcove that jutted out into the street. This section wasn't at all spacious and was kept as the private area; it had an open fire and much friendlier seating. There was a tiny door tucked away to the left of the bar and William presumed it to be the entrance to the rooms for rent above, if, in fact, that is what they were.

As William waded through the light crowd that were hovering in the narrow space between the bar and the nearest available seating, he noticed peoples' faces fall away from him like dominoes.

'Hi there, I wonder if you could help me?' said William, as he advanced through the Barrel's population that evening. 'I'm looking for Riddle Manor.' But with unrivalled rudeness, the faces span in any direction that wasn't William's.

'Pardon me, sir,' he continued. 'I seek directions to Riddle Manor? I've come to see Lily Jayne.'

Nobody knew him, yet nobody was willing to offer him any assistance. Instead, the inhabitants of Weepers Hollow were quick to shy away, either hiding behind their stout-filled glasses or pretending to be already deep in dialogue.

'Can anybody help me?' shouted William, surrounded by the Hollow's most ignorant denizens.

He heard mutterings about him and fragments of conversation but whatever the locals were talking about, they had no intentions of sharing it with William.

William felt what it was like to be unwanted and it carved him up like the rancorous gale that was setting in outside.

Despite feeling the communal will of the locals sending him away, William pulled up a seat at the bar at the same time as two gentlemen collected their drinks and moved in the contrary direction.

As he sat down with his back to the crowd, he eyed the selection of drinks that were lined up just an arm's reach away. He quite fancied a glass of mulled wine and a hot meal, but there was no barman or landlord to be seen, nor heard. William was rather confounded for a time, as everybody else in the tavern had drinks and they surely didn't all help themselves.

As he looked about the cosy interior of the pub, William noticed a shady male character peering out from behind a door that was tucked away beyond the bar. As William spotted the man looking towards him, the figure stepped back rather abruptly and out of sight.

'Sir! Hello? I'm talking to you, sir, back there. May I get served?' William bellowed.

The man remained hidden for a moment before giving in to William's persistence. He crept out from hiding with a cold, stale glare. Not a single inch of his face moved and his obedient, greying hair sat heavy upon his head. He had a rather broad forehead and these sharp, jagged ears that underpinned his personality. The way he moved reminded William of how he imagined Frankenstein's monster to move: slow, calculated and full of menace. His arms dangled by his side and at the end of them were two tightly closed fists. He wore a buttoned up white shirt with sleeves rolled up on both sides and a casual waistcoat, which he left open.

'How may I help you…sir,' said the landlord, cuttingly, while standing firm and upright. His face was focused, giving testament to his intensity.

Somewhat startled by the man's stiff, piercing tone, William took a gulp of air and took his time in coming to answer.

'Good evening, I'm William,' he said, while offering to take the man by the hand.

'Yes,' replied the landlord, shunning William's attempt at a handshake.

'It's bitter out there,' said William, retracting his gesture. 'I'm sure glad to be indoors.'

He wasn't actually that glad, as it was probably just as bitter inside as it was out.

'May I get a glass of red wine?' said William, once he had realised that the landlord wasn't given to much small talk.

After a few seconds, the disgruntled barman broke his icy contemplation and without asking his preference of vintage, proceeded to pour William's drink and slide it in front of him, peering at him through his bushy eyebrows.

'Is there anything else...sir?' Again, the quality that made William's palms sweat returned. The way he voiced 'sir', clean, crisp and eloquent, yet shrill and overly earnest, came with a tinge of resentment and much later than the rest of the sentence, almost out of obligation.

'Yes. Do you serve food?'

'The kitchen closes at nine o'clock...sir.'

'And are those rooms I see above?'

'We have no rooms available. Now, will that be *all*...sir?'

The man was tiring of William's questions already and instead of asking about the Manor, or even for his name, William thought it best to be out of questions, as the man frightened him somewhat and made his skin crawl.

In that moment, a hatted man, who had evaded William's earlier attempts to gain assistance, brushed by and planted a folded note into William's pocket.

William turned his gaze to watch the man out the door, not once glimpsing anything but the back of him. While the landlord still awaited his dismissal, William retrieved the note, which read:

Outside. 5 minutes.

There was nothing at all traditional in the man's handwriting that suggested to William that he was much past thirty years old; the letters were fancy but in a modern way, not the kind that you might associate with someone who was perhaps any older than that. William ran a finger over the ink and, as skilled as he was in the written word, he could tell that whoever left him the note wasn't a stranger to the pen. It even occured to William that the writing was strikingly similar to his own.

'*Will that be all?*' said the landlord again, unpleased to be kept waiting.

'Oh. Yes. I beg your pardon. That will be all for now, thank you.'

'Good evening to you then…sir.' The landlord rolled his eyes and proceeded to take his leave.

William had no idea why he was requested outside and the shifty way in which he was summoned unsettled him. However, after processing the situation and deciding to trust this stranger as being his only hope of acquiring assistance in such a peculiar place, William softly stomached the remainder of his wine and headed outdoors.

As he stepped from the bar into the entrance where his belongings were held, William heard the local drinkers erupt into busy conversation again; it was as if closing the door to the bar behind him was a switch of sorts.

As he dressed in his coat and hat, William savoured the last few moments of warmth before stepping out into the wind that sang out behind the door, reminding William that it was still there and in force.

He exited the pub and, like earlier that evening, the place was as dead of life as the tavern was of manners.

From the shadows emerged a man's whisper.

'Psst. Willy Boy. Over here.' A thick heavy arm reached out and waved from the shadows that coloured dark the alleyways beside The Slaughters Barrel.

William was lucky to hear the sound over the fierce wind and he followed it happily into the darkness, all the while wondering why they had to hide their encounter.

CHAPTER ELEVEN

Stanley Garrick

In a blackened corner of Weepers Hollow, Mr Stanley Garrick offered his assistance in carrying William to Riddle Manor. Garrick's proposal was sharp but William didn't mind the brevity of their first encounter. He felt a great sense of urgency to go about his business as he had already wasted half the day chasing his own tail, or so it seemed, and was rather pleased with the idea of making haste at last.

Garrick was a shady character. If it weren't for the nervous way that he kept twitching and peering out from the shadows as if hiding from the law - or something much worse - William would have put their sheltered meeting down to the passing wind that would have no doubt whisked away their words before they could be heard.

Garrick's character was misleading. The man conducted himself in a manner that suggested he had at least sixty years behind him. But the way in which he spoke, in an odd accent that William took to be the local one despite it not matching that of anyone else he'd heard speak, revealed that he was a man who was still in touch with his youth. His words were playful and jumpy and they bounced off his tongue like a rabbit in springtime.

The bridge of his top hat casted a rather prominent shadow on the upper half of his face and William asked himself how well he could trust someone whose eyes were kept hidden, as he knew all too well what that meant. Garrick was a big man, beefy in stature with enormous, raw-looking hands to suit.

Before a few minutes were up, Garrick checked the coast was clear and darted out from hiding, hands anchored deep into the pockets of his dark suede coat and his collar flaps already wrapped around his neck.

William was not permitted to follow him. Not right away. Garrick made William agree to wait a brief while before following in his footsteps. William didn't like to ask questions, after all, Garrick was doing him a service that he was already most grateful for.

Despite the oddity of it all, William felt comfortable enough to trust the man; there was something strangely familiar about him, but William couldn't quite put his finger on it. After what William considered to be a brief while, he, too, leapt from the shadows and hurled himself in Garrick's direction with a pace that was, if anything, quicker than that of his new companion.

Following Garrick's directions, or rather what he remembered of them, William had walked briskly for what felt like half a mile or so before veering left down Goldstone Crescent.

The street was littered with trees either side and branches reached out over the road and met in the middle, forming an archway of sorts. It was all rather protected and private, but that's exactly what Garrick was going for - privacy.

At a close distance, William saw Garrick sat in the driver's seat of a horse and cart. There was a cloud of smoke in the air above his head. He had a pipe in his mouth that wasn't there before and which became his defining feature. He was curled up in his clothes, waiting rather anxiously for William to join him.

A strong black horse with blinkers played chaperone to Garrick's trap. It was a marvellous beast and it looked to be treated much better than the animal that bowled over Mr Caine and sent his medicines flying. Its mane was trimmed to perfection and its fur was as smooth as Indian silk, although only by sight, as William hadn't dared lay a hand upon the imposing steed. As William drew nearer to his ride, he couldn't help notice how focused it was. This was clearly an obedient beast.

William felt just how focused the horse was when he climbed aboard the trap. He hadn't lifted both feet off the ground before the horse was pulling away; which was more the fault of Garrick, as his instructions to advance came promptly and prematurely. For a moment, William worried for his life. There was a flash of unbalance and uncertainty, and as brief as it was, William nonetheless had time to imagine himself falling off and being trampled under those heavy hooves; a thought that he didn't like to linger upon for too long as it made him shudder somewhat. He wanted urgency but he didn't mean *that* kind. In the height of William's insecurity, Garrick reached out to catch him and with a firm tug on his jacket, managed to nestle William safely into his seat.

As he sat gathering his nerves, William noted that there wasn't much room for a newborn baby to sit beside Garrick, not least a fully-grown man; but he wasn't about to complain, for the cosiness of it was the least of his worries.

For some few miles, Garrick never spoke a word. Instead, he whistled to himself between puffs on his pipe, strangely content with the silence.

William thought it rather bizarre that Garrick would help a man without knowing what his business was. What William found even more bizarre was just how it was that anything could be that far away in Weepers Hollow that they would be travelling for what felt like a lengthy while.

The place was quite inwards and, on first impressions, looked to be a place where you could wake, sweep its perimeter and return home in time for breakfast. But then William recalled his aimless trudging on his arrival and accepted that it was perhaps a larger dwelling than he had first thought.

As the cart rode through the Hollow, the driver was caught up in the present and William was caught up too, but in his surroundings. In the silence, save that of the trotting of hooves, the wooden wheels and the windy call of the nighttime, William soaked himself in the short supply of splendours that Weepers Hollow had to offer in its desolate state, all the while playing out in his mind his reunion with Lily. There wasn't much to look at though, not just because the night was dark, but also because it was empty; it made perfect sense to William to call the place Hollow.

As a way of passing the time, William entertained himself with a game of guessing the horse's name. His first thought was Jasper, though he didn't quite understand why - at first glance, the animal just looked like a Jasper. *Or was it a Rocky? It's certainly masculine enough to be. But then again, it's too well groomed for such a hard name, so maybe not Rocky, perhaps something majestic like...Duke. Yes, Duke. It has to be.*

In the rare quietness of his mind, William speculated, and quite excitedly, too, the name that Garrick had bestowed upon his charger. But before long, it occurred to him that although it was quite amusing, studying the characteristics of the animal and passing guesses as to its label, how would he, in fact, know whether or not his deduction was correct? The game suddenly wasn't as much fun anymore, and so William thought, should Garrick decide to speak at any time, that he was to stick with Duke.

They had come out into a countryside clearing and Weepers Hollow lay behind them, quiet and self-contained as it was. William's head lurched at the surprising beauty - the broad, bare openness of it all. The sense of space and the immensity of the sky above, dotted with stars, as it stretched over the moors as far as the eye could see, appealed to him greatly. He felt as if he had lifted his head above water when the Hollow was drowning him. It was his time to breathe clean air, air that was untainted by the sinister aroma of the place.

'There's no direct road up to the Manor, y'see.' At last, Garrick spoke again, yet William wondered what suddenly compelled him to do so.

'I beg your pardon?' William detached himself from his stargazing and replied rather quickly in the hope of latching onto Garrick's efforts at making conversation.

'You're curious as to why we're travelling so far out the village. It's because there's no direct road up to the house. Not for...not for my loyal steed here,' said

Garrick, using the mouthpiece of his pipe to point to the beast as if William had somehow missed him.

For a brief moment, William thought that Garrick might have spoken the name of his horse, but the way he evaded it was as if he wanted to keep him waiting.

'I see.'

'My apologies for the hastiness back there, boy.' Before William could even begin to ask about Duke, Garrick spoke again and he was thankful for it. 'We can talk more freely now that we're away from the prying eyes of the town folk.'

'Don't mention it, no apologies necessary. I'm just grateful for your help. I hope you don't mind my asking, but the townsfolk you speak of, they did seem rather worked up about something?'

'Oh, I wouldn't pay much attention to them, Willy. They're just narrow-minded people, y'know?'

William didn't like to be called Willy - he considered himself far more sophisticated than to have his name reduced like that - but he sensed that the air between him and Garrick could quickly turn sour should he have corrected the man.

'It's all rather neighbourly around here, y'know, in Weepers Hollow. Everybody knows everybody and when a stranger steps in, oh, they just go *crazy.*' Again, Garrick whisked his pipe in the air around him in some visual aid to his speech.

'I see. It's just that I rather formed the impression that it was something personal - something aimed at just me.'

William pushed for a more substantial explanation, or more accurately, the truth.

'Well like I said, boy, don't go paying any attention to that lot. In fact, you're probably best off without their company, and their conversation for that matter.' Garrick no longer spoke with a bouncy intonation. He was much more serious, for a moment at least, as if his words were not his own.

William got the impression that Garrick was hiding something from him, as he was behaving in the most mysterious manner. Not only was he unsmiling, but he was adamant not to speak in detail of the townsfolk.

Suddenly, William was thrown into Garrick as the horse took a sharp right turn, which naturally marked the end of William's curiosity and his probing for answers.

William was able to sense the renewed strain that the beast was under, a strain that meant that they were climbing ground and were on course to reaching the hilltop where stood Riddle Manor, cold and alone.

The remainder of their journey was filled with routine chatter - sparks of conversation that was neither here nor there - which gave William the opportunity to feel around Garrick's ambiguous temperament and which brought the two closer into each other's trust.

CHAPTER TWELVE

Riddle Manor

The air had grown hostile and the bitter cold cut through William like the land cuts through the ocean.

William stepped nervously from the cart but soon wondered whether he should retrace his steps; the imminent storm was plenty enough to reason a retreat, let alone the chill that suddenly rang true inside his bones.

The night was darker without the glimmer of the street lamps in the village below and the trees swayed violently in a wind that was much more vocal on the hill than down in the valley; the setting had rather reminded him of a recurring dream he'd been having.

'Will you be alright from here, boy?' From his tone, William could tell that Garrick wasn't at all that enthusiastic about hanging around from fear of being engulfed by the mysteries of the night, and in fact, couldn't help but thinking that the offer came only out of obligation.

'That's awfully kind of you, but I think I can manage from here. Besides, I feel I have imposed upon your time too much already.' William had wished that he would stay but likewise felt an obligation to let the man go about his next business.

'Out of curiosity, may I ask what is it you expect to find here?' said Garrick with wide eyes fixed upon him in anticipation of a response.

'I shall be fine,' said William, as he nervously looked about him before wondering into a night shrouded in secrets. 'You go on ahead. Thanks again.' The way William ignored Garrick's question was as if he hadn't even heard it.

Before Garrick could speak again, the thick fog swallowed William and his curiosity. He pushed through into a clearing untouched by the mist that was steadily closing in around Riddle Manor.

Convinced that he was in the wrong place, William pulled the letter from his pocket and took one last look at the return address, which, to his disappointment, matched the inscription on the crooked and barely hinged gate that gave entry to the grounds of Riddle Manor.

He turned back hoping to see Garrick, but the smog had already consumed the driver along with his cart and carrier.

'Garrick?' William called out, not for a response, but more to remind him of his own company.

He pushed through the gate and cautiously proceeded along the gravel path, which leads up the hill to a grand entrance. The thud inside his chest reminded William that his heart was still there, though terrorised as it were.

The house itself stood alone upon the hilltop with a retired menace, as if it had been exiled from the village some years ago; it certainly had the rancorous frown for it. There was something about the way the front-facing windows and door were composed that made it appear as if a human face, staring out over the Hollow and scowling through both sunshine and rain. It was white against the black clouds and boarded windows faced in every direction, marking the structure as it began to sag in its old age. Skeletal branches played peek-a-boo from behind the daunting edifice, almost too scared to come out. The front door, pale in colour to match the patchy paintwork of the exterior, hid beneath an archway that was approached by rather questionable steps.

Everything about his location gave William the impression that something wasn't quite right, but the letter told him otherwise.

With every step he took, the sensible half of William had wished it was in the opposite direction, but the thought of seeing Lily again carried him ever closer like it did that day in the park. He remembered how his feet took charge and, like that day, William trusted them. There was this energy pulling him towards the house coupled with a compulsion not to turn away. William had no idea what it

was but whatever was interfering with his free will felt…
supernatural. Though he felt an otherworldly interference,
William didn't have the audacity to pause and to question it.
He thought that if he threw any attention to the strangeness,
it might just consume him, cripple him, even, to the point
where he would never find Lily.

With the ageless pull of winter by his side, William
advanced on the house, leaving the howling wind behind
him; it dared not follow him up to the house. As he arrived
at the steps, he took one last look down the hill in search for
Garrick, but all he could see was the empty dirt track where
the gentleman had left him.

As he turned back, he noticed that the front door was
already ajar. *Lily must have got my letter,* he thought. *But how
could she have known I'd be here at this time?* He inched open
the thick heavy door and its screech killed the already dead
silence.

Inside the house, there wasn't a single surface untouched
by a lavish layer of dust. William was even leaving footprints
in the grey powder that stretched out over the floorboards
that rest beneath the feet he had perhaps misplaced his
trust in. A tired, yet majestic staircase ran up the right side
of the Manor's interior, and to the left was a corridor that
gave passage to a row of uninviting rooms. Immediately
to the left, though, was the living area, crowded by a grand
piano that was collecting grime from the tense air. At the
foot of the staircase was a Victorian cabinet embossed

with gold hinges and handles remarking the family's wealth, and a once-red carpet layered the floor of the living room, skipped over the portico, and spanned the stairway.

Although the wind was too scared to advance on the house, the fearless fog had crept through the open door and reached up the steps, as if marking the way for William to proceed. There was that compulsion again, the urge to move forward as if he was being stalked by a wolf of the night.

As he moved through the hallway, William felt something other than the dust spreading beneath his feet.

He tilted a look to the floor and gathered in a pile were a number of letters. He knelt down and upon closer inspection realised that they were, in fact, his letters. *If Lily didn't get any of my letters then this has to be the wrong place?* William questioned, while somewhat relieved that he wasn't just simply being ignored.

He scrolled through the countless unopened posts that filled his hands, before throwing them back down and suffering the avoidable cloud of dust that returned the favour in his face.

Suddenly, he heard a distant thud. It started off soft and steady. Rhythmic. Da-dum. Da-dum. He strained his ears to listen. The noise was coming from upstairs. Fear began to grow inside him as steady as the morning. Here was a house clearly uninhabited, yet he heard noises. Strange noises. Noises that begged for an explanation.

William reached for a candle that was placed atop the cabinet by the entrance. As he went to strike a match, he noticed, much to his displease, that the candlewick had already burned out. Instead, he lit the first match and proceeded with the rest in palm, except for one that he slipped into his inside jacket pocket.

Although removing himself from such a putrid place was the obvious option, it had occurred to William that perhaps it was one of Lily's sick jokes, and that maybe it was her payback after the despicable way in which he had treated her of late. It *would be a little extreme*, thought William, but he so desperately wanted to believe it.

With that fixed in his mind, and with the first matchstick nearly out, William decided to follow the fog's lead up the grand staircase.

Chills ran down his spine and then back up again. Out of pure fear of the unknown, he called out for Lily, hoping with everything he had that she would reply.

With each step he took up the stairs, the thud got louder. Da-dum! Da-dum! The fact that *nobody* was answering his calls unnerved him, especially when he was expecting Lily to come running. He had already visualised how it would all play out and this wasn't it.

'He-llo? Who, who's there?' said William, in a voice impaired by his own anxiety. 'I'm look-ing for Lily.'

Occasionally, William would fall into darkness before stumbling to light a fresh match with trembling hands. He was a cautious visitor, sick to the stomach with a sense of impending danger. William's skin tightened around stiff bones as if he were the next guest at a dinosaur's dinner party.

At last, he reached the top of the stairs. He felt as if he had just climbed Mount Olympus, but lacked the sense of personal achievement.

The second floor opened up to a long narrow corridor that was lined with three doors on either side. The moonlight shone from underneath a door at the far right end of the walkway.

With only an evasive flame for comfort, William moved closer to the sound that was all the while getting louder. Da-dum! Da-dum!

As he crept by the other unopened doors, he dreaded to think what he might find beyond them. Fear had completely taken over. He glanced back to see that even the fog dared not edge any closer. He was on his own.

'Lily?' William called out one last time, but he already knew it wasn't her. With false daring, he pushed on. The tiniest sounds that occupied the silence between thuds grabbed his attention: the creaking of the floorboards, the whistling wind outside as it howled at the walls warning William to turn back, the heaviness of his own breath and the relentless beating of his heart, as it pounded away in his chest as if wanting to bail on him like a tempered beast caged against its will.

The fire cast William's shadow on the wall and made him feel like he wasn't alone, yet he knew better. He was so close that his flare had fused with the moonlight that pushed through the door.

The thud was at its loudest. DA-DUM! DA-DUM! The noise wasn't just louder but faster, too. It sounded like a train passing by his face at a dangerous speed.

With a matchstick on a timer, William edged even closer to the door, scared of what he was about to find behind it.

The flame danced to the rhythm of his unsteady breathing. He took one deep breath. With the strength of a turning tide, he twisted the handle. Punctuated by a stroke of thunder, he swung the door open. A huge gust of wind rushed through an open window and attacked the matchstick, sending it to sleep. In the corner of the room was a rocking horse swinging frantically in the streak of moonlight that shone through the window.

The toy was fashioned out of red wood, which glistened in its varnished condition. Stale black eyes spied through a thick and even blacker mane that curtained the horse's narrow but gentle face. Its body was smooth and well maintained and across its back was a fabric saddle embroidered with the name Abby.

William's skin shivered, as he found nobody in the room there with him. Besides Abby and an empty cushioned chair that was angled towards the window, the darkened room was, like the Hollow itself, empty.

William was suddenly aware of every sensation. He stepped up to the rocking horse that was showing no signs of slowing down. He reached his hand out to stop its swing. At the same time, a wrinkly hand with crusty, elongated fingers reached out from behind and rested gently upon William's shoulder.

Stunned by the touch, William turned in a flurry of panic. Amidst the fuss, he collapsed to the ground, folding like a bad poker hand. He swiftly backed away from the figure in front of him and showed no embarrassment in clinging to the wall like an infant boy clutching his mother's leg.

William looked up. The moonlight sat gently upon an elderly lady dressed in a sour white gown. Her appearance sustained William's frightful emotions that had already started to bleed through his veins. Supple leather skin stretched over the figure's frail skeleton. Her elongated face jutted out from a nest of grey vipers and her broken teeth, thick with the colour of rotten yellow, jarred against unusually pale and ghostly pelt. Her garish eyes were forward, yet uneven and her right eye had seen better days judging by its sore expression; *it was like looking into a pool of molten magma*, William thought. The wrinkles that masked her body cut so deep they were more like scars.

'Hello, William,' said the woman.

CHAPTER THIRTEEN

The Questionable Truth

The moonlight didn't follow the lady as she stepped from it and edged closer to William. Her walk was as crooked as a bolt of lightning, and with each step she took, the fearing wreck on the floor moved back, pushing so hard against the wall that kept him there that he might just have pushed through it.

He felt the sweat drip down the side of his face so vividly he could count every bead. William was paralysed by dread with nowhere to run.

'Who are you? How do you know my name?' said William, wrestling the words from his mouth.

'I am Lily,' said the ghastly woman. 'Don't you recognise me?'

'You're not…you're not Lily. Lily is…young and beautiful, you're old and frankly, quite frightening.'

'Oh now, there's no need to be scared of me, my dear.' Although she spoke with niceties, hate still lived in her words and William could see it, the coldness in the flame or her conversation.

The lady turned away from William and shuffled over to her chair. He came to ease slightly, now that the arresting figure no longer loomed over him.

'Tell me who you are then?' said William.

'I told you many times. I am Lily.'

'Lily Jayne?'

'Yes.'

'You liar! You're not Lily,' shouted William in a temper, as he hit his fist up against the wall. Fear had been replaced with fury and frustration as William tried to make sense of what was happening to him.

'Look, Lily has blonde hair. Blue eyes.' He retrieved a worn photograph of her from his pocket. 'The most beautiful thing you'll ever set eyes upon. See?' William held the picture to her. 'And you're not her!'

'Get up, William. Get to your feet and stop embarrassing yourself.'

William didn't need telling twice. He, in fact, wondered to himself *why* he was still hunkered on the dusty floorboards. William returned the photograph to its home and stood, ridding his clothing of soot as he did so.

'Who are you really?' said William, tired of the games.

The lady stared out of the window and the fog had cleared enough for her to see the village below.

'You know, this used to be a decent place. The streets were crawling with friendly faces and the air was light, so light,' said the woman, while William listened on intently. 'It was as if the place had been ripped from paradise itself. And it was my home. I made lots of memories, lots of wonderful memories. Weepers Hollow was more than a village. It used to have character and it was a friend. But it was wronged and now it's gone into hiding, refusing to come out for anyone. What you see out there now is nothing more than the devil's dumping ground.'

'Why are you telling me all this?'

'Do you know what that's like? To have paradise snatched away from you like that?'

'I'm beginning to. What happened here?'

'You happened, William. You happened.'

There was a long, uncomfortable pause; a moment where William thought he was talking to a mad woman, a cynical old sow scorned by love and doomed to live out her days in solitude like Miss Havisham.

'Wait. What have I got to do with anything? Who the hell are you? And don't you dare say Lily.'

'I was Lily's grandmother,' she signed. 'She was given my name.'

'I thought you were supposed to be sick?'

'Yes. I was sick. I was extremely sick, in fact. But now I'm not, and I feel no pain.'

'Well, that's great. So, where's Lily? My Li…wait, what do you mean you '*was*' her grandmother?'

The lady looked to William with eyes that had suddenly softened and glazed over, while her body remained as hard as the lines on her face.

'Where is she?' Although William felt something in the air, something downright ugly, he could never have predicted what he was about to hear.

'Lily *died* three years ago, William,' said the woman, punctuated by another sigh. 'You of all people should know that.'

'What? No!' William's entire demeanour, from the swaying of his head in disbelief to the wagging of his finger, denied the woman's assertion entirely.

'Yes. She's dead, my dear, and you did that to her.' The lady spoke with a shade of resentment.

'No. You must be mistaken,' said William. 'I was with Lily just a month ago. We received a letter, written by your hand, requesting that she visited you in what you believed to be your final days. And now here you are telling me she *died*, and three years ago, no less? No. I'm sorry, but no, I am not accepting that,' said William, as he looked around him with his hands resting coolly upon his hips. 'So, wherever she is, you can tell her that the game's over now.'

'She's dead, goddamit! How many times do I need to tell you, child, before you accept it?' The lady's hands trembled in time with her legs as they rested on the arms of her chair. 'I summoned her here because I was dying, but instead, it was my sweet, *sweet* Lily who died – and I need to carry that burden with me for eternity.'

'I still don't believe you. I mean, I don't even know you,' said William, as he continued to shake his head in disbelief. 'How is this possible? Explain that to me.'

'No. It's painful to talk about it. Especially with you.'

'What's that suppose to mean: especially with me?'

With every word that William dared to utter, the lady grew icy and bitter. She turned away, and with her gaunt fingers, pointed to the door.

'You should never have come here. You should leave. Find your peace, William, and don't come back next time.'

'I want to know the truth. I deserve to know the truth.'

'You deserve nothing.' The words she spoke felt like they should be shouted, but there was something even more poignant, something downright scarier, in the quieter way in which they were delivered to William's ears.

'I've come all this way to see the love of my life, who I have been away from for over a month now, and the least you can do is tell me the truth. You owe me that much.'

The lady did well to keep her cool for a time, although William could sense her bubbling like a volcano and wondered how far he could push for answers before she would erupt.

'I owe you nothing. Besides I've already told you the truth, you just refuse to accept it.'

'You told me she's dead. That's it,' said William, as he began to grow furious and pace around the room. 'I'm just supposed to take your word for it? Just believe that I'm never going to see her again? Tell me, what kind of sick game are you playing here? And say it is true - which it isn't - but say it is, right? What kind of lover would I be if I just neglected her like that?'

'That's exactly what I keep asking myself.'

'I don't believe you,' William seized his frantic pacing and stood still in front of the woman. 'She can't be dead and you know what? I'm going to find her.'

'I suggest you start at the graveyard,' put in the lady, intensely and with spite.

'Enough! Now listen, Lily, or whatever your name is, I want the truth.' William grew tired of her lies and in a bid to acquire her full attention he took hold of her chair and twisted it away from the window. 'She met Eddy, didn't she? And she's asked you to cover for her. I knew it.' He spoke with confidence as if he had figured it all out and everything suddenly made sense.

The mention of Eddy seemed to do the trick and William was taken aback as he watched the volcano spew its molten guts. She leapt forward out of her chair with inhuman vigour and glided effortlessly towards William as if she was carried by the wind and weighed nothing at all. Before William knew what was going on, he could smell her stale breath as it raped his face; she was so close to him that he could see the hairs creep from her nostrils.

'Now you listen to me, child, and you listen carefully. Lily is dead! You will find her in the graveyard. Now get out of my house.' Although she spoke slowly, her tone was ice cold and it sliced right through William like a well-placed length of steel.

The lady had a degree of sincerity in her pain-filled eyes that made William *almost* start to believe it.

'If she was buried, why wasn't I invited to her funeral?' William was frightened to ask any more questions, but he was so troubled and perplexed. Hurt, also.

'Get out. I won't ask you again.'

William stepped back out into the corridor, which grew incredibly dark after he had closed the bedroom door behind him.

For a while, William stood staring at the other doors wondering if Lily *had* found her way back into Eddy's arms and was now hiding in one of those rooms. It seemed to all make sense to William: the unopened letters, the distraction of the grandmother and Lily's supposed death to keep him forever at bay. It was all speculation, of course, which came out of William's utmost refusal to accept this nightmare as reality.

William, ignoring the woman's orders to leave her house, moved to the closest door and with conviction, twisted the handle, only to discover the door had been locked. He did the same thing with the remaining four doors on that level, all of which were also locked. He thought about breaking down the doors, but only for a second before dismissing the idea, as he didn't like the thought of further upsetting the woman who had already made her will so crystal clear.

William hadn't even left the house before he could hear the heavens open up. The rain smashed onto the tiled roof with as much ferocity as a wave crashing against the rocks.

He reversed his route through the shadows of the interior with a limp drag as if his body was seconds ahead of his feet. He stepped over the letters and out of the house, not closing the door behind him, but leaving it ajar as he found it.

The fog cleared to take cover from the rain, but William found the lashing water soothing, as it washed him and his grubby thoughts.

What do I believe? It can't be true...can it? With every ounce of him, William didn't want to believe that his lover had been torn from this world and the more he turned his mind on uncovering the truth, the more it evaded him.

There was but a single way to lay his doubts to rest and that was to pay a visit to the cemetery. So, unprepared, William dissolved into the night, making his way to the home of the dead.

CHAPTER FOURTEEN

A Grave Attempt

William navigated his way around Weepers Hollow and to the cemetery, which was situated in the heart of the Whispering Wood; a six-acre plot tucked away behind the village and out of sight of the everyday goings-on.

Although there were no directions from the Manor, William found his way to the graveyard with considerable ease, as he had remembered sighting the plot while travelling out of the village with Garrick. He distinctly remembered the cemetery, as it seemed to harbour a darkness of its own that was unlike the darkness that consumed the rest of the village.

The rain had softened considerably and was thinking about stopping altogether, but was rather unlikely. William thought that the rain eased only to catch its breath and await reinforcements.

Owls hooted from the treetops and the fog had sneaked out from hiding to conceal the cemetery in a film of secrecy.

William knew that, with the thick mist returning at a pace, it would surely be hard to find Lily's tombstone, if indeed there was one. Not quite ready to confront the possible reality anyway, William made the easy decision to retreat back to The Slaughters Barrel where he could give up for a while and gather his strength.

Although he hadn't received a pleasant visitor's welcome earlier that evening, the warmth and food, which the tavern promised, would go a long way towards settling his erratic nerves.

CHAPTER FIFTEEN

The Bottom of the Barrel

For the second time that evening, William found himself at The Slaughters Barrel. This time, he stepped through the entrance with a little more conviction than previously, as he already knew what to expect from the townsfolk and was even made defiant by it.

After hanging up to dry his hat and coat, he approached the bar where the landlord, who made no efforts to hide from him this time around, had a glass of red wine waiting for him. William wasn't too bothered about the other drinkers and, in fact, chose to show as much negligence towards them as they showed him some few hours ago.

There was, however, someone who William couldn't help but direct his attention towards. Over his right shoulder was a young and beautiful woman making conversation and laughing with a good-looking man of about the same age.

The woman was as beautiful as Lily and it saddened him so. She had the most exquisite hair, long, wavy and golden to threaten the sun. She was so mesmerising that he could hardly steal his eyes away from her – there was something in staring at another woman and remarking her attraction that awoke William's guilty conscience.

This woman, who was stood on the cusp of the Barrel's private area, was completely unaware of William being there. As he stared at her, a tear fell from his eye; he remembered the last time he had seen something of such epic beauty, and it pained him ever so.

William watched on as the woman caught sight of a man wading his way through the crowd in her direction. In the blink of an eye, her gleaming smile had morphed into a grim expression; she was scared.

William couldn't quite make out the man's face through all the bodies in his way and this particular punter pushed through them as though they didn't even exist.

From what William saw of the man, he was brawny in stature, although that was more from the confident way in which he ploughed through the crowd. He had this intensity about him - an intensity that suggested he might have been the aggressive type. The only other detail that William could make out from where he leant against the bar was that the man had dark, well-groomed hair. He was hoping to get a look at his face but was denied at every opportunity, almost as if the man didn't want William to see him.

He approached the woman like he knew her quite well, but it appeared that he was in no mood to issue any form of gentle greeting. Instead, he grabbed her sharply by the arm and peeled her away from the man who she had been conversing with.

From where he stood, and considering the volume of chatter that evening, William couldn't make out what was said, but whatever it was didn't go down well.

Before the woman could say a word though, her bold evening companion stepped in, presumably to her aid like the type of chivalrous gentleman that didn't seem to exist anymore.

The aggressor broke his firm grip on the woman, leaving a nasty trace on her arm, and in the same motion, swung a tight-fisted punch, knocking down the concerned fellow and miraculously breaking not a single thing in the process, besides that of the gentleman's nose perhaps.

Somewhat shaken by the violent turn of events, the fragile woman turned away with the intention of leaving the Barrel. But with his hefty arm, the bar's bully kept scooping her back against the wall like he was swatting a fly – each time with a little more force, which reflected his growing frustration – and she began to look like a soft toy in the grizzly grip of a dog's mouth. The sight of it angered

William to the point where he felt his own blood boil with familiar rage. He grew upset, too, and a tear formed, once again, in the corner of his eye.

He twisted a look around the interior of the tavern and it was as if he was the only one seeing this poor lady being abused. Everyone else was contained in their own little worlds, deliberately shielding themselves from a confrontation that so evidently scared them.

William was afraid, too, but not ignorant. He was silently willing the man, whose back had been turned on William the entire time, to stop and to just leave her alone. For a moment, he even considered acting out, but there was something about the man that unseated him and made him tremble with unbridled fear. It had nothing to do with the way he levelled that gentleman who had already stepped up to him and who was now creased over on a bench, clutching his face and avoiding any further beating. Instead, in spite of his own rage for which he knew not how to handle, William shied away like a turtle in its shell.

His father taught him that the eyes are a gateway to a man's strength, but William didn't care to look into another man's eyes for fear of what he might find, or what other men might find when they looked back into his. He harboured secrets deep in his very being, secrets that he wanted to give away to no man.

William avoided confrontation for that reason alone. It wasn't courage to step toe-to-toe with another man that he lacked, rather it was the courage to show himself for who he really was - to give another man a window into his soul and into his primitive self.

On the surface, William was a good person, but he also knew what he was capable of. He was afraid of what another man, who was geared up for war, might stir inside of him, what it might awaken, for he knew that when the fire raged inside, he could truly hurt someone; and for William, there was no better reason to unleash his inner demon on a man who had glimpsed his deepest and darkest secrets.

With women, it was different because no matter what happened, William liked to think that he could never hurt a woman.

'That man is bad news,' said the landlord of the aggressor, whilst towelling glasses and minding his own business. 'And if I were you, I wouldn't keep staring like that.'

Although William was staring at the man, all he could see was the back of him, so broad that it eclipsed the lady he was abusing.

'I feel like I know that man,' said William, breaking his intense gawking and turning back to face the landlord.

'Of course you do…sir', said the landlord, unsurprised. 'There's not a man, woman or child in the whole of Weepers Hollow, or within a radius of at least one hundred miles who doesn't know that man by now. He's not quite right in the head. He did something unspeakable some years ago.'

William wasn't listening to the landlord as he droned on about the man of whom he was so obviously frightened, as was everybody else in the room. Instead, he took a sip of his wine and subtly glanced back over in his direction with penetrating eyes.

By now, the woman was in tears. William could see them arguing, but couldn't quite make out what it was about. In a viscous, but provoked outburst, the woman slashed her palm across the man's face and dashed for the exit, careful not to bump into anybody in her erratic departure.

In a fashion that seemed to fit the man's demeanour, he swiped a stiff drink from the clutches of a lonely nearby senior and glugged it down without a moment's care.

With a bang that went largely unnoticed, he slammed the empty glass down on the tabletop and took his leave in pursuit of the woman. As he did so, William quickly turned away, worried that their eyes might meet. Although it was his chance to see what this man looked like, William hunkered down over the bar top, concealing himself as he stormed out, with as much, if not more conviction and ferocity as he had when walking in.

Throughout the incident, William thought it was extraordinary how not a single set of eyes, save that of his own, was put upon this vile chauvinist and the mood appeared to lighten the moment the man had stepped out.

For a minute, William thought about how he could just sit there while that poor lady needed help and when nobody else seemed to care.

'Eddy doesn't come in here much - once a year, maybe - but when he does, there's always some sort of trouble,' said the landlord to himself, but loud enough for William to hear.

'I beg your pardon, did you say Eddy?' said William.

'Yes. I thought you said you knew him?'

As he realised who the man was, William was suddenly flushed with rage. He had suddenly departed with concerns of exposing himself in confrontation, but in that rage, he felt a moment of hope. As painful as it was, William clung to the idea that Eddy knew the truth of Lily and he was prepared to do what he must to get it from him.

William found himself torn between an impulsive desire to rip Eddy to pieces and a yearning for the truth – or more accurately, a version of the truth that he could accept.

In a bid to take the edge off of what he was about to do, William bellied all that was left of his drink, threw a fleeting wave to the landlord and with the taste of rich burgundy wine upon his lips, marched for the exit.

The landlord's eyes followed William out the door while his head subtly swayed in disapproval.

William didn't waste any time coating up, for the weather was the least of his worries.

William exploded out of the Barrel and onto the street. He staggered for a moment, frantically looking about him. Although he was only seconds behind Eddy and the woman in exiting the pub, neither of them was anywhere to be seen.

Weepers Hollow stood in front of him in its most typical state – a ghost town. William surveyed the dark passages that veered off in every direction and, for a short while, considered walking into the night in pursuit of the man who he harboured an incredible and deep-seated hatred for.

The wind and rain were still in force and looked to stay.

As he stood gazing into the distant darkness, William suddenly fell under a daze that rocked him to his core. It wasn't an attack from any physical being, but an attack from within, and it came like a train driving through his gut. The feeling was so debilitating, he crumbled to his knees, all the while staring at his hands and crying out into them. As he caught his reflection in a puddle beneath him, he drove his fist into the ground as if he couldn't stand the sight of himself.

Exhausted by his own rage, William fell to the ground. It was as if the rain itself was the thing beating him from the way his body collapsed, one limb at a time, until he eventually levelled with his face pressed against the puddled paving.

As he lay there in the cold rain with the moonlight upon his back, his body began to shake violently.

Given the quiet place that William knew it to be, there was nobody around to help him, and so, with the flood for a nightcap, his eyelids wrapped around weeping eyes rich with pain.

CHAPTER SIXTEEN

Rise and Shine

Throughout the course of the nighttime, the wind rose. As William lain half sleeping in a bed that belonged to The Slaughters Barrel, wondering how he got there and what that terrible pain was that he felt in his hand, he had become aware of the sturdier gusts that blew every so often against the windowpanes. It had increased greatly in force like a ship at sea abused by the gale that came roaring across its sails. The glass panes rattled in their cases and there was the sound of whistling through all the cracks in the building.

The noises didn't bother William so much, but what did unseat him was the thought of the monster that was shaped like a man. Eddy burned at William's mind and he warmed his hands on the blaze. It infuriated him, and as he rested there, trying to calm the rage that turned somersaults inside, he reflected on how much he wanted to hurt him. It was a peculiar desire he felt and was rather out of character for William - to want harm someone so badly that he found himself constantly wishing for it, his blood boiling at the thought of it. With that cutting away at his mind, William drifted back to sleep, falling deeper and deeper to the sound of the wind at his window that was booming, but powerless to reach him.

In the height of his slumber, the old dream crept up on him again like a predator on its prey. The dream was much more vivid than usual. The deep red of Lily's blood was so highlighted it was as if he was dreaming the rest in black and white.

The sharp sound of a door slamming sent shudders rippling through William's room and called him out from his tainted sleep. It had barely turned six o'clock in the morning and his premature awakening was far too abrupt for William's liking.

For a while longer, he was happy to slip back into the pleasant state somewhere between sleeping and waking.

Later, after having slept for what felt like a week, William awoke to a sunny morning. As he went to lift his head, he was suddenly aware of the heaviness of it and of the pain that it was causing him – he couldn't remember drinking that much the night before but the sensation of an unrelenting hangover was what it felt like. As he raised a hand to his head, he noticed his knuckles were bloodied and bruised and no longer was the pain he felt a mystery.

William forced himself to rise and as he sat up, he gently stabbed his thumb into his palm in a bid to regain some feeling. He noticed that his clothes were hung over the heater and although they looked dry, they were grubby and William tried desperately to remember what exactly happened to him the night before; but it seemed that the harder he tried, the more the memory was lost to him.

As he sat stimulating the dormant muscles in his extremities, William heard screams coming from outside his window. He drew back the curtains on a pale blue sky, and although the screams were getting louder, he saw nobody beyond the glass. The sound was immediate as if there was somebody there in the room with him. The view from his window was so unobstructed by people that William thought perhaps the screams were from afar and what he heard was the echoes that were carried over the hills.

William took a hot bath and although the warm water eased his body's tribulations, his mind was still plagued by the screams from the outside. At one point, William thought he could hear a woman cry for help, but the volume and pitch of the shriek were all he could focus on as it reverberated between his ears.

As he slipped deeper into the bath with only his head above the surface, William felt his temperature rising and his blood boil beneath his skin. Steam lifted from the bathwater at the same time as beads of sweat trickled down William's cheeks. He soaked a flannel in cold water and sprawled it over his forehead; it was like putting out Eddy's fire that was now burning away at his face.

He stepped out of the tub with as much enthusiasm as when he had stepped in, pleased for his body to cool and reset to room temperature, which was warmer than usual.

After his attempt at relaxation, William began to feel less depressed about the day ahead and like the pleasant weather that filled his room, he allowed himself to feel hopeful.

As the daylight was burning, William made haste downstairs, which was completely devoid of bodies, save that of the landlord who was wiping down the tables after a night filled with peculiar antics.

With more of an appetite than he had anticipated, William sat and pondered the breakfast alternatives on offer that morning. As he did so, he was aware that the landlord was yet to acknowledge his presence and it was now up to him to grab his attention if he had hoped to eat anything at all.

As the sun shone through the window and reflected off the landlord's forehead, William found a natural way to strike up the morning's conversation.

'Lovely morning?' William said in a volume louder than what was perhaps necessary.

'Indeed. I hope to get out for a bit of it later on myself, but I don't expect it'll hold out that long,' the landlord replied without paying much attention to him and whilst setting the appropriate volume for chatter.

'Thanks for last night,' William said, trying even harder to acquire the landlord's full attention. He had assumed that the man had played a large part in finding William to a bed and was glad for it; although somewhat embarrassed, too, as such disorder was out of character for him.

'Don't mention it. I've learned to expect that sort of thing around here,' said the landlord, as he finally turned to face William while noticing the luggage that had accompanied him downstairs. 'Heading home so soon?'

'If it's OK with you, I hope to have some breakfast here first before going…running some errands in the village, then yes, I shall be bound for my home.'

For a brief while, the landlord just stared motionless at William with eyes that suggested that he wanted to say something to him, but for some reason, couldn't. The silence was so marked that it prompted William to issue a verbal prod in his direction.

'I mean, if it's a problem, I could skip breakfast?'

'No, no, don't mind me,' said the landlord, coming out of his contemplation. 'What is it that you were after?'

'A bowl of oats and some fruit perhaps?'

The landlord nodded.

William found his comfort in a corner of the tavern, which had a rather pleasant view out over the village. He bathed in the sunshine that shone through a large window, ready and waiting to receive his breakfast.

With his breakfast, William was handed The Daily Weeper to read while he came to grips with his duties of the day. As the newspaper passed hands, the headline 'Local Girl Brutally Killed' that was strapped across the cover, grabbed William like a shark in shallow water. William was so traumatised by the headline that he allowed his oats to grow cold while he digested the full story.

By the end of the article, the newspaper was shaking in his hands. His imagination was cruel as it ran amuck with the thoughts of Eddy. He knew nothing of anything, yet he was adamant that Eddy was to blame for the nighttime atrocity.

The heavy-laden guilt returned to his conscience, guilt that came from not putting a stop to the man before he was too late.

William was so stunned by the horror of what he had read that he closed the newspaper and debated running away from the place he wanted nothing more to do with. He liked the idea of crossing paths with Garrick once again, but instead of carrying him up the hill to Riddle Manor, he would request safe passage to the edge of the world where he could jump off and just free fall into the abyss.

Just as unconcerned with the rest of the day's news as he was with his breakfast that had begun to turn clumpy in its neglect, William threw The Daily Weeper on the table in front of him and swiftly rose with a degree of agitation that he could have done without.

What William hadn't realised, in his rattled state, was that the newspaper was dated 2 September, 1909, three years ago.

A Grave Matter

'You'll find Weepers Hollow a quieter place today,' said the landlord, as he noticed William leaving and came to see him off.

'Quieter? That's a laugh. It's been a ghost town ever since I got here. Well, all except for that screaming out there this morning,' replied William, while layering up for the outside.

'Screaming…sir?'

'Yes. Surely you must have heard it? The sound was so distinctive that I wouldn't be surprised if it awoke even the dead. Which reminds me, I have those errands to run,' said William, while edging himself closer to finally taking his leave. 'Thank you for your hospitality, I can't say whether I'll be back again – to be honest, I shall be rather glad to be leaving this place.'

'Yes,' said the landlord. He stood with a blank expression for a moment before angling his gaze towards The Daily Weeper that William left upon the tabletop.

Conscious of the fact that time was approaching the afternoon and not wanting his spirits to become so depressed that he might have begun to be affected by all sorts of morbid fancies, William took his leave and began making his way to the graveyard, with his appetite lost and belly empty.

As he went to step out the door, William paused for a moment before turning back to address the landlord one last time.

'That young girl in the paper, it never said her name. Who was she?'

'I don't know…sir,' replied the landlord, but William knew that he was lying.

'Not the lady abused in here last night, I hope?'

'Again, sir, I can't help you,' said the landlord unflinchingly. 'Perhaps ask someone in the town?'

'Right. Yes. Right. Will you be attending the funeral?'

'Oh, the whole of Weepers Hollow will be attending, Mr Hardy. There's something about a grim gathering that the village folk find irresistible,' said the landlord, while reminding William of his monotony. 'I mean, they'll be free food and drink at the wake.'

'I see,' said William, stealing a solemn gaze to the ground.

'Will I see you there, sir?'

'No!' said William. 'I mean, no, I haven't been here all that long, so I don't think I quite qualify.'

'Yes. It's probably for the best that you don't attend... sir,' said the landlord in a serious tone that was quite distinct from his usual drone, like a warning almost.

William's soul felt crushed by the weight of the innkeeper's tenor and with caution, nodded his goodbye and finalised his exit.

'It was good to meet you,' called the landlord after him. 'again,' he added, but to himself.

The weather was rather pleasant, so pleasant that William thought he might have woken up somewhere that wasn't Weepers Hollow. But the emptiness of the streets and the smell of something rotten meant that it had to be.

On his solitary walk to the graveyard, William didn't like to be left alone with his thoughts, but rather had no choice. Something was going on his head that he couldn't quite explain, and it could have been anything: the wine, a night of interrupted sleep or the festering thoughts of Eddy. All he knew was that it hurt him.

William yearned for closure so that he could get back to the place he called home. But to do that, he knew he first had to confront the possible reality of finding Lily in the ground.

Although the distance was greater, now that he was traversing it on foot, than it seemed when he trotted over in Garrick's cart, William found the graveyard with relative ease. The place looked much different in the daylight, naked almost, as what is a graveyard without the darkness for an accomplice?

From the way it ceased, it was as if the harsh weather, that was beginning to seem rather customary in the Hollow, didn't know that William had a job to do - for surely if it did, the rain would rally in with its army of foggy foot soldiers, just to prevent William from doing what needs to be done.

As he cautiously stepped through the graveyard, William became suddenly aware of the task at hand and how finding a tombstone, which may or may not be there, would be like finding a needle in a haystack, or worse even, as at least he knew the needle existed.

In every direction, rows of tombstones stood erect in silence forming a sea of the dead. Some were crumbled with the weathering of centuries, and some were smooth marble with black writing laid with floral tributes. Most, though, were overrun and dishevelled, for now, even their mourners had joined them under the clay soil. Upon the hill, a new grave had been dug and was awaiting its tenant. A spiked fence, suitably black in colour, marked out the perimeter of the graveyard like a prison. The smell of old stone and stale soil filled the dry air like sand filled the desert. Gravel paths, most of which were invaded by greenery much in need of a manicure, gave some navigation around this myriad of people held firm in the earth's embrace.

Just under an hour had passed and William was beginning to feel like he had been tricked and sent on some wild goose hunt for the amusement of others; he believed it too, as it was often the case that he was made to feel like a joke. And although it was tiring, it was all good news for William, because no grave meant that the woman who claimed to be Lily's grandmother was lying and that his lover must still be alive.

Somewhat exhausted from circling the cemetery and sick to death of reading dozens of simple obituaries, he parked himself on a patch of ground, which had escaped being dug up, and took a quick look around him for prying eyes before disrespectfully leaning back against a conveniently placed headstone.

William slumped there picking at the grass between his fingers and feeling like the whole world was laughing at him. As he did so, he felt a bitter breeze cut across his cheeks that made him feel cold. He thought maybe it was time for him to be leaving, as he wasn't expecting the kind weather to hold out quite as long as it did, let alone for much longer.

Readying to leave the place, William rose to his feet and there in front of him was a headstone that read:

HERE LIES LILY JAYNE.
BELOVED GRANDAUGHTER.
BORN 1880. DIED 1909.

Although he had seen already a magnitude of stone markers, none brought him as much unbearable pain as this one did. He felt the wings of tragedy rush against him, and it hurt – it hurt badly. He was alone, ejected from life like a bullet from a gun. He met the devil, and she was dressed in white. She came and tore his heart right out of his chest, only to force feed it back to him while laughing in the most sadistic tone.

As spots of rain began to litter the air, William began to sob like a child at the sight of Lily's headstone. He was rendered powerless to move from where he sat. William felt so constrained that it was as if the rotten corpse six feet beneath him had reached up through the generous layer of dirt that separated them and held him firmly in place; William likened the agony to what it must feel like to be tied down to a rack whilst having his limbs stretched to the point of dislocation.

We all find angels in our hardest hour, but not William. There was no angel for him. Not now. Not after what he had done. All there was for William to turn his mind on was guilt that fell like rain – and lately, it had been pouring down.

William buried his head deep in his hands and rocked back and forth to the ebb and flow of the unbearable pain that consumed him. He then lowered his hands and wrapped them tightly around his chest in a squeeze, trying desperately to comfort himself and ease the emotional torture.

His cries split the heavens in two. His cheeks were stained with the endless stream of tears that fell from his glossy eyes. He sat there, alone, enduring the hurt that continued to engulf him.

To a clap of thunder, the heavens opened, and rain spilled heavily over Weepers Hollow. Although he was soaked through and through, William had hardly noticed the rain, as his mind was so far from meeting.

Once the human carcass had released its grip from upon him, William waded on his knees through the wet mud to Lily's grave and embraced the ground beneath which rested his Lily. He could feel his heartbeat pounding away against the hard ground, but that's all it was – just one heartbeat.

Just like that, William's world had been turned upside down, and although he found answers, he also found more questions. The possibility of it all being one sick joke had faded like a forgotten memory, and William now had to deal with the reality of never seeing his beloved sweetheart again.

Once his sobbing subsided for the time, William dried his eyes that were now sore and wide. His cheeks were pale and lips dry, despite the torrential downpour.

From his coat pocket, William pulled out a tiny black box, in which was a gold wedding ring, patterned and with a round diamond in its middle that sparkled in every imaginable colour.

There was a question that William wanted to ask Lily. It was the same question that he wanted to ask her the night she left him on their anniversary. The question tore at him now, and, as he gazed down at his lover's resting place, he was almost motivated to speak those very four words. They rested heavily upon the tip of his tongue, but in the end, William swallowed those words, as he knew how much it would hurt him when his intended said nothing back. Instead, William rested the opened jewellery box upon the top of the headstone, closed his eyes and sat waiting for his nerves to settle and wits to gather.

As drops of rain landed upon the ring, they turned to blood. The blood then dripped down across the face of Lily's headstone and ran in the grooves of her name.

William found something soothing in being outside in the rain. It was almost like it came just at the right time to cleanse his body and mind. In a place so riddled with the dead, the soggy lashings upon his skin reminded him that he was alive.

In a hurry, the drops of blood had dissipated before William opened his eyes. With his body moving on memory alone, he staggered to his feet and collected his belongings.

With his luggage in hand and void of any vigour at all, William stepped back up to Lily's headstone, kissed his hand and touched it upon her name.

Something then tugged at William's attention. It was the dates that were so finely etched in Lily's stone. The numbers affirmed the frail woman's words as they echoed in his mind:

"Lily died three years ago."

To William's utter frustration, seeing this did nothing but further heighten his confusion. *Could it still be a joke?* William thought. *It must be.* William was determined that he was the subject of somebody's amusement, as he was so assured of his recent reality.

He rubbed a hand across the dates, hoping that the chunk of stone would crumble to his touch and disappear along with the hurt. But sadly, there were no illusions here for William, and he was soon back inside his mind, completely at a loss.

William took back the ring and returned it to his pocket before making his way out of the graveyard, bound for the station and with the recent revelation weighing heavy in his broken heart.

In his tracks, William was, yet again, halted by something. He paused. *It can't be.*

With a rush of *something*, he turned back, and planted there beside Lily's headstone was another, almost identical, but which read:

HERE LIES LILY JAYNE.
BELOVED MOTHER AND GRANDMOTHER.
BORN *1829*. DIED *1910*.

What greater punishment is there than life when you've lost everything that made it worth living?

-WILLIAM SHAKESPEARE

CHAPTER EIGHTEEN

Empty Corridors

William left the graveyard like something that had just been dug up. Numb. Lifeless. He felt heavy and sick in his mind, stale and exhausted and rattled too, his nerves and imagination were on fire.

All that governed William's thoughts now was how, all of a sudden, his life had morphed into something utterly meaningless. He felt but a pale shade of a man, haunting a world fallen from concern. Where was Garrick to deliver him to the edge of the world? This time, instead of plunging himself into the black, he would soak God's creation in gasoline and gladly lay a match to it. And, after watching the earth set ablaze, he would willingly step into the flame and burn with the rest of it.

Outside, everything was silent, so that all William heard was the steady sound of his footsteps as he began to walk across the gravel paths that lead out of the burial ground; even this sound, as quiet as it already was, was softened the second William struck out over the green.

Some minutes later, it was hard to tell just how many, William snapped out of his reverie to realise that the thunderous rain had pulled back on the reins - although it no longer mattered, as he was already soaked and couldn't get any wetter, colder or more depressed - *perhaps that's why the skies dried up*.

The daylight wick had almost burned out, and the skies were morphing into a darker shade, as the sun entered into hiding. If there had been any daylight remaining, the incoming mist would have scarcely allowed it to penetrate the foul misery of the atmosphere.

This wasn't just any mist and certainly wasn't the kind that William was used to receiving back in Mane. It was thick and damp and encased everything in its sight. Even William felt lost in it. It was fine yet dense, and constantly on the move. It choked and blinded, smeared and stained. It had the smell that you'd associate with the musky pages of an old book - the colour, too; yellow and filthy. It was so clingy that it was as if it were built up of millions of tiny insects that scuttled all over him before going along their way.

William's mind was numbing once again, trying desperately to replicate the feeling that manifested itself within the rest of his body. But despite the touch of nothingness, he trudged on through the veil of mist like in a game of Blind Man's Buff, trusting only his memory and unproven sense of direction to return him to the Manor, despite the fact that he didn't want to be going back there.

He had secretly hoped that, in walking blind through the blanket of smog that concealed this strange place, he might end up in the fresh and untainted countryside, a mile or two in the opposite direction with his back turned upon such a ghastly place; a place that was teeming with all sorts of things that did nothing but hammer away at his soul like a blacksmith pounding away at his creations.

Although the thought of leaving Weepers Hollow in the fog cheered him up to the point where the severity of his situation became lighter to bear, William wasn't about to run away. Instead, he decided to push on in the direction of the house, for the woman whom he met there only yesterday had some explaining to do.

William knew that he was drawing nearer to Riddle Manor, not because he could see it, because he couldn't, but because he could feel it, somewhere in his bones as they tightened once again.

With nighttime drawing in at a pace, William wondered just how long he had spent at the graveyard that suddenly an entire afternoon had been swallowed up.

After a tiresome trek that felt considerably longer without Garrick's horse and cart, and his company for that matter, Riddle Manor, in all its miserable glory, stood erect in front of him like a forgotten lighthouse expelled from the coast.

With renewed purpose, William took those last few steps up the hillside to eventually be met with a familiar door, already ajar, just as he had left it.

He stepped through into the entrance hall, completely unsure of what to expect given what he had just witnessed in the burial ground. He was, nonetheless, still keen to meet the woman with whom he had spoken the night before, whoever she was.

'It's William. I've come back,' he shouted, a lot less frightened this time. He immediately proceeded up the staircase towards the room where he had left the woman said to be Lily's grandmother.

Although the day was growing dark, there was still enough daylight to hint at the interior of the house, providing a comfortable degree of visibility as he moved with a touch more conviction in his return.

'Hello?' He gave voice to his presence once again as he drew nearer to the room at the end of the corridor.

The time it had taken for William to transition from the front door to the room upstairs felt a lot quicker than previously, as William wasn't so cautious this time.

'I've been calling you...' William swanned into the room, but to his surprise, it was empty of the woman.

The furniture, including the rocking horse and the chair in which the woman sat, had been concealed by dust sheets that appeared to have been untouched for years by the way they had collected dust. The window that once gave passage to the moonlight was now boarded up, too.

Suddenly, William felt dazed and confused, yet again, and questioned whether there was something in the air around Weepers Hollow that coloured him so; it seemed that that's all he ever was in that place - confused.

William turned and stepped from the room, closing the door behind him. As he did so, he heard a noise. Da-dum. Da dum. It was the same dreadful sound that he heard the last time he found himself in that god-forsaken house.

William stopped dead in his tracks. He glanced back at the closed door. The sound ripped through his body, rendering it numb with fear. With aggression, his heartbeat rose and the sound now matched that of the one that unnerved him. Tormented, William edged closer to the door. He laid a suddenly moist, shuddering hand upon its handle. He slowly creaked the door back open to see Abby, the rocking horse, violently swaying on its own beneath the sheet that gave it hiding. In its disturbance, dust lifted from it like smoke off a fire.

Motivated by the frustration that came with his lack of understanding, he stepped aggressively up to the moving toy and snatched away its cover. As he did so, he hoped that the woman would reveal herself again, but in a kinder, less startling manner than she did the night before.

William looked around him, expecting her to appear from somewhere, but all was as dead and quiet as the grounds for which he had just come.

After scouring the room for the woman and being somewhat disappointed by her absence, William noticed something different about Abby - something worrying that pierced right through his false bravado and formed a stubborn lump in his throat.

The toy was still red, but no longer glistening. The once-rich colour had faded so much that it made the horse appear as if it had been skinned. The stale black eyes had been plucked out of their sockets and replaced with tiny pieces of mirror glass into which William didn't like to look for too long. He used to recognise himself, but it's funny how his reflection changed. A thick black mane concealed the horse's now sharp and sorrowful face. There were knots carved into the body as if it were victim to some brutal assault.

The longer William looked upon it, the more violently it rocked. William's heart rate rose, and his breathing grew more and more frantic. He was dizzying now. He could feel the sweat congregate around the pores of his forehead before dripping into his brow. His palms felt hot and clammy, too.

Suddenly, in a tempered flurry, William covered the horse and stopped its oscillating motion.

William's fear triggered the boldness within him. With aggression, he searched the rest of the house, room by room, for the woman, or at the very least, for signs that the house was still occupied.

As he approached the first door and remembered that it was locked, he prepared himself to drive his shoulder through it. He plastered his grip upon the handle and began to turn it. As he threw all of his body weight into his attempts to break the locked door, he fell through it, as the door wasn't locked after all.

The room was bleak and bare. Its minimal furniture was covered, all except a writing desk that had its own dustsheet crumbled by its feet. William's love for writing nearly compelled him to cover the desk back over, but the invading powder had already taken it like pestilence takes people.

After madly stumbling through doors and empty corridors, he found neither of the things for which he had been searching.

CHAPTER NINETEEN

Hardy & Heward

Stepping slowly and cautiously from the house, William invited a welcomed change of pace from darting across its interior and falling through the empty corridors like those in his mind. He trod over the letters that were piled on the floor and pulled the door, not closing it, but leaving it ajar as he found it.

The outside was foggy, to which William could relate. This didn't trouble him much, as, if anything, William considered the thick fog to be his only friend in his troubled time, with Garrick of course. He helped the fog to perform its duty of masking everything in sight by deliberately stepping into it.

William found something strangely gratifying in submitting himself to the smog that disguised the unfamiliar world. It surrounded him so that he was unable to see even himself, and he liked that.

As he stood bounded by the stained air, William felt as if he were in the clouds and despite the matters that burdened him so, he felt as light as the clouds. As he observed the mist float in the air around him, he, too, imagined he was floating, unshackled by the sharp, heavy objects of his mind and free of the guilt that held him there.

Although the putrid air wasn't at all pleasant, it wasn't bad enough to stop William from allowing it to fill his lungs as he attempted to compose himself once again.

After calming his mind to a degree in which allowed William to continue through his harsh reality, William set off down the hillside towards the village where he hoped to catch the return train back to Mane.

It wasn't running away. William assured himself of that. Though there were questions left unanswered, he convinced himself that he had found some shade of closure in witnessing Lily's resting place. In those thoughts is where he found shelter from the truth, and it made giving up easier to bear. William felt tired. Tired of there always being a riddle in his head, always something to question over the way things came to be.

Parts of him felt like he should stay and continue his hunt for coherence, but what good would that have done him? All the matters in which he had faced there already were altogether terrifying, purely because they were so intangible and inexplicable, incapable of clarity yet so deeply affecting. It was as if everything was conspiring to kill him and he felt quite at a loss to continue coping with any of these things. Although William didn't get what he came for, he got enough to warrant his retreat.

In the cover of night, William made his way down into the village. As he did so, he willed the legs that were to carry him home to stay strong and not to give up on him just yet.

William staggered through the vacant passages of Weepers Hollow and the deafening noises in his head jarred against the deathly silence of the streets. He was hardly near the station, but his weary body was already on the brink of shutting down.

He felt dried up and parched from racing throughout the place, and exhausted, too, from the emotional rollercoaster that he was riding. A dull throbbing nestled into the left side his head, just behind the brow, as if something firm was pressed there. The ache looped around his ear and down to the base of his neck; it was too early to tell, but it felt to William a lot like the routine migraines he had been experiencing sporadically for some years now.

William's pace grew slower and slower with each step forward, and eventually, he came to a halt. His body wanted desperately to give in, whereas his mind was happy to continue its torture. His eyes began to twitch and grew sore as sweat dried around them. Prompted by the irritable itch, he rubbed his eyes, which only made them worse and which disturbed his vision.

As he stood in desolation, weighing up the dichotomy of body and mind, he looked up and through blurred vision, saw Eddy standing outside a grocery shop that was just across the street.

In the shadows, Eddy stood in the window of the grocers looking in William's direction, but not seeing him. Although the shadows darkened his face, William could swear that it was he, waiting in the darkness like a predator of the night, smug and over-confident.

Under any other circumstances, William would have allowed the sight of the grocers to take him back to his childhood and to hold him there for a while. His uncle's friend Arthur Tombs had owned a grocery and every Saturday, he would make up a bag of food for William's family and would always put in some coconut ice for William. The sight of Eddy rocked him too much, and it wouldn't spare him a few minutes down Memory Lane.

As he stood there with the adrenaline fuelling his tired limbs, he felt provoked to attack. He wanted to drive his fist so hard into Eddy's face that the sound of his bones breaking upon impact would be trapped inside his memory forever.

William's fists tightened by themselves and he felt the crunching of the bones in his hands as they did so. Heavy with tension, his arms dangled by his side and his feet found a new lease of life as they readied themselves to march into battle.

William had set Eddy in his sights, but he had barely had the chance to step down off the paving before he heard someone call out his name and which drew him out from his trancelike state.

William retreated from his plans in fear of there being a witness to what he was about to do. The shout was heard over the hefty sound of trotting hooves that could only have belonged to one horse.

'Evening, Willy Boy,' declared Garrick on approach, and in his usual, distinctive voice.

'Good Evening to you, Stanley,' replied William, through an audible sigh.

'What were you looking at there, boy?' asked Garrick in the most curious manner, as he attempted to trace William's gaze.

'Packing in for the night?' said William, completely ignoring his question.

'Oh no. Not yet, boy, not yet. He's a big old beast is Troy and he needs his exercise, isn't that right, laddy?' said Garrick, hurling his tongue at the horse.

Finally. Of course it was called Troy. What else? The horse was so big and so powerful and the strength of the Greek army may just have lived within.

'We've been held up in the barn most of the afternoon, you see, on account of the dreadful weather. I figured I'd let him tire out before I tuck him away to bed,' continued Garrick.

'I see.'

'You're heading back to the station already?'

'Yes. How can you tell?'

'You've got your luggage there,' remarked Garrick, pointing down to it with the tip of his pipe.

'Apologies. It has been rather a long day, and my mind is far from meeting.'

'Well climb aboard, boy. Let Troy take you there?' said Garrick, holding out a hand. 'Looks like you could do with a rest.'

After a few moments of hesitation, William leapt aboard the cart. He returned his hateful gaze to the grocers to see that Eddy had disappeared. William figured that Troy must have frightened him off, for he was terrifying enough for it if you didn't know him.

William knew that there must have been a good reason Eddy kept escaping his wrath as he did, and it was frustrating; it was like playing football, but every time William took a swing, the ball moved. It was probably for the best, as William wasn't quite ready to give away the secrets of his soul. Besides, deep down, he wasn't a violent man, but he feared that Eddy would make him so, and there would be no coming back from something like that. Not again.

CHAPTER TWENTY

The Hollow Station

With a whip of the reins and a stern 'yah', Garrick issued Troy the signal to advance. As the cart pulled through the village, William kept looking around him, focusing his sights on the web of dark spaces that may have given hiding to the monster who had evaded him for the umpteenth time already.

Garrick was silent for a while, and in that silence, William remarked, once again, the beauty of the beast that pulled them. He was drawn to the sight of the horse's fine muscles as they pumped under the skin like a machine. There was something in the way that Troy moved that reminded William of a shark – always moving forward - and he took note, as there was certainly a lesson to be learned in that.

William's thoughts lay as heavy as the horse that carried him away. There was only so many things that he could distract himself with before those thoughts crept back into his consciousness and returned him to the darker corners of his being. He hoped that Garrick would keep him engaged in lighter, more trivial matters, as he knew he had plenty of time to be alone with his volatile deliberations on his lengthy and dreaded journey home.

'Did you find what you were searching for at the Manor?' Garrick spoke as if something suddenly provoked him to fill the growing silence.

William was happy to talk about anything - anything but that.

'I did. Thank you again for getting me there safely,' said William. 'Your kindness has made my time here a lot easier.' William thought that telling a lie was the only way to shut down a particular line of conversation for which he had no desire of pursuing.

'Nonsense, boy, don't mention it,' said Garrick, with a fleeting swipe of his pipe. 'I must admit, I felt rather embarrassed when nobody in the Barrel had offered their assistance.'

'Yes, I found that rather bizarre myself, even in a place as...unconventional as this,' said William, choosing his words carefully so as not to offend the only person who didn't make him feel alone. He continued, 'But might I ask, why were you so secretive in offering me your aid?'

William was pleased to be leaving chatter of the Manor and the purpose of his visit behind them like the dirt that Troy flung from his hooves.

'It's the people, you see. They can be cold. Critical. It took me long enough to earn their trust and approval and I wasn't about to let you ruin that for me, boy.'

'Why do you need their approval?' said William, unbeknown to the way of the Hollow.

'Unlike most of the other folk, I wasn't born and bred here, didn't grow up through the ranks as it were. So to them,' he said, while taking pause to puff on his tobacco, 'I was an outsider. Just like you. The Hollow can be a lonely place to outsiders.'

'I found that one out for myself.' said William, begrudgingly to himself, but loud enough for Garrick to draw some sense from.

'So I am sure you'll forgive me for wanting to keep my allies in check.'

William nodded quietly in agreement.

'Why did you move here, anyway? It's not exactly an idyllic destination?' said William, looking about him and remarking the drabness of the outside. 'Not for foreigners of the place like you or me.'

'At the time, I had nowhere else to go. And believe it or not, the Hollow was a pleasant place back then.' Garrick sat back and sunk into his seat, letting go of all the tension in his previously taught body. One hand hovered his pipe inches from his mouth, the other rested on his knee while loosely gripping the reins. 'I picked up this cart, cheap enough, and began driving people wherever they wanted to go. This work does well to keep Troy in good shape and gives me a chance to become one of the locals as it were. I could meet people without appearing invasive. Quite strange, some of them.'

'There's still something I don't quite understand. How is it that you came to be in a place like this to begin with?' William was happy to hear Garrick's story, so long as it meant not having to talk about his own. And fortunately for William, Garrick was just as happy to tell it.

'Well, boy, some years ago, I travelled this way to purchase Troy at an auction, just a few miles north of here,' said Garrick, in a voice that demonstrated higher levels of energy than that of his limp body. 'We were riding back through this place when Troy got tangled up in the boggy marshes on the outer edge of the village. We managed to avoid the thick of it, but Troy's front leg buckled to the point where he was unable to walk…well, he could walk, just not far. Not without it causing more damage, y'know?'

William looked again to Troy and could never have imagined such a well-built specimen ever weak and vulnerable.

'So why didn't you just head home when Troy recovered?' said William, plainly, as if Garrick hadn't already thought of that himself.

'Feels strange, y'know, talking about me like this,' said Garrick, peeling his eyes off the road every so often to meet William's keen regard. 'Usually, everyone who sits in your seat just wants to talk about themselves. Y'know, I'll tell ya, the number of times I've nearly fallen asleep in this seat from the dull tales that climb aboard. People never seem to get that I'm a person, too, with feelings, experiences and… it's like, to them, I'm just here to provide a service. I move through the streets, largely unnoticed, until someone needs me. Then, suddenly, I'm the ears for all their troubles to fall upon.' Garrick shakes his head to himself, rattled by his own rant.

William said, 'It's a pity your so called *allies* don't take the time to get to know you better.' Garrick slipped him a look to say that he was right. 'But please, sir, go on.' William was quick to set Garrick back into discussion before he would attempt to turn the tables and want to learn about his life.

For a moment, Garrick was lost for where his story had left off. He fixed his face in a way that revealed his perplexed trail of thought and which prompted William's aid in reminding him of it.

'You were about to tell me why it was that you did not just return home?'

'Oh yes. Well, yes, boy, that was the plan. But while I left Troy here, in the care of a few kind locals I might add, I travelled back home only to discover that I didn't have a home to go back to. Oh the bastards!' said Garrick, as his face crumpled in angst. William was disturbed by the sound of strained leather as Garrick's fist tightened on the reins.

William was so engaged in Garrick's story that he had forgotten all about his own torment - for a while, at least.

'In my absence, a fire broke loose and ripped through my entire farm. Suddenly, I found myself with a brand new workhorse but with no work for it.'

'I'm sorry, I didn't mean to pry on painful memories.' Although William felt obligated to offer his condolences, he truly did mean it. The pity wasn't for the fact he had lost his home and possessions, but because it meant that he had to stay in a place as unwelcoming and frankly, vulgar as Weepers Hollow.

'So you just stayed here?' What about your family back home? Your friends? I assume nobody was hurt,' said William with a tone that suggested that Garrick was completely crazy to remain in such a place.

'Oh, I couldn't stay there,' he replied, defeated. 'Not after losing everything like that. Besides, the only family I had died years before I began living off the land. And friends?' Garrick forced an empty-bellied chuckle. 'That's a laugh. I thought the people who worked for me were my friends. That was until they got away with whatever they could rescue from the flames. For all I know, it was them who lit the match.' The resentment that Garrick harboured in his words in fact confirmed it. 'Oh, the bastards!' Again, his face crumpled, but this time around his pipe, as he took yet another puff and released, with the smoke, the frustration brought about by old memories best forgotten.

William felt compelled to share his own tale of friendships lost but thought it might have progressed down a road that he didn't necessarily want to go down. Instead, he crafted an expression upon his face that encouraged Garrick to continue with his story.

'Suddenly, Troy and the clothes on my back were all the possessions I had in the world,' said Garrick, absent of any self-pity.

'Don't depend on tomorrow because tomorrow can sometimes let you down,' said William, proudly. 'My mother used to tell me that. It was her strange way of protecting me, I guess.' William had no idea what to say to the man who had lost almost everything he had, and he figured that reciting his mother's words was better than returning Garrick's revelation with some dumb idle gaze.

'She sounds like she was a wise woman, Willy boy.'

William nodded in agreement, 'Yes, she was.' His gaze took a nosedive and landed in his lap as a solemn moment passed through him.

'So, it just made sense to start afresh here in Weepers Hollow,' Garrick said, picking the conversation back up from where William had dropped it. 'Mind you, the atmosphere wasn't so crazy bleak back then. It was…innocent.' Garrick wasn't convinced that innocent was quite the right word to voice, but he knew what he meant. And so did his passenger.

Nonetheless, William chased the conversation in danger of it dying out.

'Innocent, you say? Innocent of what?' William perked up from his sad reverie only to hold on to his own inquisitiveness for a while longer.

Garrick took a quick look around him, but William wasn't sure what for.; prying eyes he presumed.

'Some years ago, the village took a turn down a darker path,' said Garrick in his shell. 'Something feels rotten here now, Weepers Creepers I call it, but I haven't yet had the heart to leave this place behind.'

William said no more and returned to the quietness of his own intent. His mind began busying again, his eyes turned in their sockets as if on alert. He felt a chill that caused him to sink deeper into his overcoat.

'Shouldn't be long now, Willy Boy,' bellowed Garrick, accepting that the conversation had drawn to a somewhat premature conclusion and one that appeared to leave a sour taste in William's mouth.

'Just get me to the station so I can go home. I don't like this place much,' said William into the scruff of his collar. He was suddenly blunt in the way he addressed his driver, too.

After a heavy whip on the reins and a startling 'yah', Troy picked up the pace and the cart raced into the night, bound for the nearing station.

CHAPTER TWENTY-ONE

The Way Back

William arrived at Weepers Hollow Station much sooner than expected, but was rather glad for it, as for the last twenty minutes or so of his journey, he had been focusing on resisting the onsetting tiredness that was now getting the better of him. He had considered nodding off for a short time, as Garrick would surely wake him when they arrived at the station. But instead, William fought the temptation of a little shuteye, as he didn't trust his imagination to be kind to him while his eyes were closed; he had some vivid idea that he'd be consumed by the sullen illusions of the nighttime the second he shut the world out.

'Thank you, my friend,' said William, as he took Garrick firmly by the hand and returned to himself a friendlier disposition, while stealing a quick glance at his pocket watch.

'Whenever you need me, boy, I'll be there. It was a pleasure to be of service and I bid you safe travels from here on.'

'That's awfully kind of you.' William stepped down from the cart, apprehensively patted Troy goodbye and in a hurry fixed his luggage about his person, as the train was expected any minute.

'Until next time then,' yelled Garrick, as he waved his pipe through the air in a fleeting goodbye while William's back was turned to him.

'Oh, I shan't be…' William turned back around to address Garrick, who had suddenly vanished. 'coming back,' he continued in a quieter tone.

After surveying the immediate surroundings, it was evident to William that Garrick was long gone and he suddenly found himself alone, yet again, and where he started.

He took one last skim of the horizon in search of any company that he could latch onto for the journey home, but all was as quiet and neglected as the Hollow's graveyard in the height of winter, or anytime for that matter.

With a deeply felt sigh, William pushed on towards the platform where he was to meet the train along its return journey back to Deadman's Cross, where he would change over to the Lanky.

William pulled his watch out from his inside jacket pocket and noted that the locomotive was running a few minutes off schedule. He then wondered how much longer he would have to wait, as the moment of its arrival was now unpredictable and William was rather curious: *if something's a minute late, who's to know just how late it'll be?*

In that time, William set his sights upon the dimly lit space in the close distance behind him. Thoughts of Lily came to him like a flood and he never thought that he'd be standing there again without her.

In Weepers Hollow, he found loss and he feared what he found; feared all the lonely times to come. He wondered if today was going to be the day that missing Lily would finally be too much for him. As his time away from Lily grew, so did his yearning for her. His desire for her became a cut that would not cure, would not stop weeping. The world fell from concern whenever Lily was in his arms and William wished that he could cuddle her just one last time; but he knew that if he did, he would never want to let her go.

Inches from the platform edge, William stood and stumbled. He strode through his thoughts and heart and hated himself for being too late to bring his sweetheart home where she belonged.

William now understood that Lily was gone and once again, he was reminded that death moved amongst the living; the noiseless fiend was hard for him to bear.

From the depths of his despair came a dirty yearning to join his lover in the afterlife.

The sky was a murky plume and as he stood at odds with himself, he heard the steam engine issue its first warning of approach.

For a moment, William stared into the oval lamp that headed-up the train and glowed in the near distance. To anybody else, it may have been mistaken for a beacon of hope, but to William, it was an arrow, and he was the target. There was no life for him without Lily's touch, but what a shame it would be to stain the metal beast with blood; yet, staining the pristine coat of the Lanky would be a worse crime.

As the train came hurtling into the station, William began to inch closer to the platform edge. Although the iron lump was slowing, it must have clocked in at forty-five miles per hour at least when it passed the first entrance post to the station. It was the same train that had delivered him there - tired looking and still in need of a serious spruce-up.

William continued his measured steps closer towards the verge and beyond the markings on the floor suggesting a safe distance.

From the way in which William moved, it was as if there was something supernatural willing him forward and almost to his certain death; but again, he was too cowardly to throw any real attention to it.

The full weight of the train now entered the station, and its bellows were so loud that it must have found even his sweetheart's ears six feet beneath the ground.

William was held in a trance by a mysterious energy pulling him into the train's path. Perhaps it was his own deep-seated yearning to feel something other than guilt, something that replaced, or better yet, ended his emotional torture. Or perhaps it was something else entirely, the same something else that willed him closer to Riddle Manor.

The engine's cry was at its loudest. William moved dangerously close to the platform's edge. His toes now hung over the brink. The next step would be to his death. In that moment, he felt free. Lifted. He was able to laugh in the face of his own demons.

The train was close. Too close. Its dull horn shook the earth upon which stood Weepers Hollow.

William threw caution to the wind. His foot lifted. He toppled. At the last possible moment, William was snatched away from death's door. Garrick, who had returned to deliver a letter that had slipped from William's possession during their journey, hoisted William out of harm's way.

During their encounter, Garrick never spoke a word to William. He knew that he wouldn't gain much sense out of a man who was trying to kiss a moving train. Instead, he helped William to his feet, ushered him safely aboard the locomotive, that had since come to a standstill, and took the duty of apologising to the flustered attendant approaching on account of William's scare.

William took to the nearest carriage and through the window he saw his rescuer still in conversation with the steward, who was now more at ease. He had no idea what they were talking about, but whatever it was had brought Garrick some amusement, as he snickered and tittered away in spite of him.

William reluctantly sat on the familiar pigskin while maintaining his glare out of the window. He was attempting to make out their conversation, all the while wondering how it was that Garrick could still laugh. *How could he be so jovial? Does he not know that Lily, MY Lily, is dead?* In some selfish vein, William expected everyone to share his pain, but the world does not stop laughing when he cries, neither does it stop crying when he laughs.

Still chuckling, Garrick returned his pipe to his mouth and twisted his gaze to find William in the window.

The train pulled out of the station, leaving the place behind like a bad smell. Not only was Garrick staring at him, but William felt as if the Hollow was staring at him also; it was the kind of deadpan stare that said, 'We'll meet again.'

William felt like something that had been belched from the bowls of the place - churned up and awash with its rancorous stench. The pain that he felt was nothing more than a reminder that he yet lived.

He drew the drapes, shutting out all that was behind them. The carriage was darkened but still had the dim glow of an interior carriage lamp that hung from the ceiling. Streetlamps beyond the curtains shone through into the carriage and the flashes of light haunted him like roses in a graveyard.

It was a tiresome and emotionally challenging time, but at last, he was bound for his home. He was so beat that comfort came against his will and all of a sudden, he was aware of the burden of his body as he sank as deep into the cushioned seat as the stiff material would allow.

He pulled a flat peak cap from his case and lowered it over his brow, which, if nothing else, gave him a place to hide from the streetlights that burned through the carriage window. He put his weary feet up and had no qualms in saying goodnight to the day that had lead him there.

In his sleep, William dreamt an old dream of Lily lying limp on a bed of blood whilst the cold darkness closed in around her. William moved in to kneel down beside her and as he did so, Lily awoke from her death to smile up at him.

The light of dawn was streaming through the drapes that concealed him in his carriage when the thunderous sound of people on the platform outside awoke William from his exhausted sleep.

He had arrived at Deadman's Cross and was ready to change into a more comfortable carriage, as his body had numbed during the overnight trek west and now cried out for a little relief.

As William traversed the platform, the Lanky rolled into Deadman's Cross Station in its entire splendour, immaculate and on time, too. The other train soon departed; it wasn't too good for its ego to be seen side-by-side with the majestic Lanky.

William couldn't remember the last time he was surrounded by so many people and yet he felt lonely. All the laughing faces conspired to single him out in the crowd.

He waded through his fellow travellers and alighted the Lanky with familiar ease. William was secretly overcome with joy at the sight of the carriage that was to carry him home that it was as if he had seen a lake in the desert after days of treading sand.

The station was much busier than that of Weepers Hollow, and Mane also. It was the connecting point between those bigger, more industrial cities that his mother bore hatred for.

William looked at all the people busying themselves on the platform and he wished that, just for a moment, he could part company with his reality and be as easy as those seemingly free spirits that he observed beyond the glass.

He so desperately wanted to shake the world off his shoulder and leave all the broken bits to the breeze before he returned home, but they still plagued his mind with unrivalled persuasion.

With plenty of time to burn and feeling somewhat revitalised after his deep slumber, despite the numbing that was gradually easing, William decided that he would pen his mind's tribulations, the things he wanted to say to Lily, but couldn't. He was the kind of writer who found it cathartic scribing his thoughts and feelings and he felt that it might unburden him somewhat:

> *It was I. Alone, I did. I was so lost in the insignificance of mine that I failed to see yours. In my mistakes, I let you slip away. Now I am better, I implore you to say it isn't so.*

> *Of late, I have been troubled by snatches of peculiar, disconnected dreams. But in those dreams, you come to me as graceful as the tide.*

> *It's in every elegance that I see your face, but painfully not in the flesh. I wonder how close to heaven I could get before the sun picks out my eyes. I'll find you somehow. Perhaps as the years get older and we're both grey and old, I'll find you walking through the park where we first met.*

> *What is left to do now but push on through? What am I to do with these embers of memories that float from the fire of this place?*

> *I know.*

> *I burn this note now so that the smoke from the flame may find you, wherever you may be.*

William retrieved the matchstick that he had pocketed at Riddle Manor and set ablaze the scribbles in his hand. For a moment, he gazed into the flame's black army as it invaded his words. As the fire began to burn at his fingertips, he dropped the parchment to the floor and laid a heavy foot over it, stamping out the carnage.

As the train chugged away, William was now at a loss for ways to pass the time. He wasn't yet tired, as he had a good sleep on the first leg of his journey and he didn't quite fancy turning his mind on any more written words.

Refusing to become shackled by the boredom, William decided to make the most of his trip across the country, as it was his first, and quite possibly his last, trip away from his local particular.

Beyond his window, he gazed upon the world and its many sights. He knew that, before long, he would be back home with only the typical vistas of Mane to fill his gaze.

Although William found looking out over the scenery a rather pleasant experience, he wished he had shared the carriage with somebody else - someone with whom he might have discussed the plentiful sights. He found that he had loads to say about them, too. In particular, the vast mountains in which the Lanky travelled through at a pace. They were huge and William imagined how dwarfed the Lanky would appear if he was to take a view from a distance. Some were chalky, some were stone and some were even disguised in the wild greenery of the land. The track was carved so tightly into the mountains that it was a wonder how the vibrations of the railway didn't rock its foundations and send them crashing down like the world in which he now aimlessly roamed.

As William remarked the sheer height of the foothills, he marvelled at how standing at its summit would provide a vantage point far greater than any that he could have imagined in his local park. He wished to know the name of these mountains, not for any particular reason, but just so he could have a reference in case he ever spoke of them. He thought if only he had a travelling companion to ask, although there was no guarantee, of course, that they would have known the answer, but the odds of them being more versed than he in the outside world was considerably high. William half debated passing guesses like he did with Garrick's horse but couldn't quite reconcile with himself the fact that he might never find out.

Nighttime crept up on William, as did the sudden tired spell that overcame him. *It's strange how doing absolutely nothing evokes a certain degree of lethargy.* The skies were growing grey and William took that as his invitation to find his comfort and to nod off once again for the overnight stretch.

*

The Lanky drew into Mane Station at half past seven, which was later than scheduled due to an unexpected delay at Beacon Hill. William was too deep in slumber to notice the delay and was rather pleased, as it was a much gentler time to be arriving back home than the originally programmed five o'clock in the morning.

Something in the air around Mane awoke William just in time for the call for passengers to disembark. William thought it rather fortunate, too, as he had no idea of the kind of places that lay further to the west, and didn't care to know either.

William stepped from the Lanky and smiled in his return to familiarity. His arrival back home was made bitter sweet, however, by the morning white mist that came in across the plain, along with its showers.

He wasted little time in heading to his apartment and as he walked the narrow, windswept streets of home once again, he found them a lot lonelier and less homely somehow than when he had left some days prior. The streets were dead, and although it was approaching eight o'clock, there was almost always some life about Mane at such an hour, even on non-market days.

It was almost as if he had brought the countryside back with him, and in a way, he had. Despite his efforts to rid himself of them, his mind was hounded still by the enigmas that came thick and fast in Weepers Hollow.

He was lost to an internal darkness and despite its beauty, William didn't see Mane as the place it once was. It was a good place to sit and remember, not so much to make new memories, though.

He relied on the village too much to lift his spirits but had forgotten that the place no longer had a spirit of its own, for if it did, it was surely broken and the destruction was certainly visible from the outside.

As he looked around his hometown, he was taken by a wave of memories, but in the tsunami, William clung only to the good ones. He remembered kicking a ball up against Mrs Lacey's flower shop with his friends until she'd come out, yelling and chasing them away with her broom. Although only a simple memory, the innocence of it and the promise of life that it held was like a float, keeping him above water in a village that was drowning in a flood of confusion.

It brought William much discomfort to see Mane be so heartless and he knew that if his mother were still alive, she would have cursed the town for closing her only son down.

The journey on foot wasn't all that far to William's apartment, but his mind and body were beat and despite the discomfort it bestowed upon him, William already longed for the easiness of Garrick's cart to carry him home.

William stumbled through the vacant passages of Mane, and in a fleeting moment, he thought he saw Troy dart across his horizon, pulling Garrick as he sat proudly in his cart. William called out, but his words were immediately lost - suffocated in the nothingness of the place. Perhaps he imagined it, but he could smell the thick body of Garrick's tobacco fill the air around him.

With the promise of warm water and fresh clothes to erase a hard journey anchored in his consciousness, the broken man owned the last few paces home, pleased for his travels to be over.

CHAPTER TWENTY-TWO

Welcome Home

William reached his apartment just after eight o'clock when the day was coming into bloom.

Before entering, he stood for a moment with his eyes shut, bathing in the home breeze and in the joy he felt, although bittersweet, to have once again returned to his trusted holdings.

The indoor air was crisp still from the grip of dawn, as the sun's warming rays were yet to break through the exterior. Nonetheless, William removed his outerwear as he advanced up the staircase, ready to hang on the rack as he stepped through the entrance to his apartment.

To the rhythm of his own footsteps, William proceeded through into his living room, setting down his travel case and moving across the room to spread the curtains and to welcome the morning into his abode.

As he moved over to the kitchen area to procure a well-deserved brew of the warmer kind, William was disturbed by the faintest of sounds emanating from his bedroom. As he stood wondering its meaning, the sound grew in volume. It was the sound of clambering with the occasional knocking of wood as if someone was attempting to climb through his bedroom window.

William continued through into the kitchen and retrieved a rather large knife, as he didn't quite know what - or indeed *who* - to find there. He gingerly approached his bedroom door, which was already ajar, and gently pressed his left hand to it. His other hand tightened around the butt of the blade.

Like a curtain being pulled back to reveal the daylight, William slowly swung the door open to reveal Lily stood in her nightgown, looking into her hand mirror and fixing her make-up.

William immediately dropped the knife outside the door and his trepidation turned to ease. He smiled as Lily looked to him.

'Damn it, Lily, I could have killed you,' said William, but to himself. 'Good morning, my dear, did I wake you?' he continued, addressing Lily in a casual manner that suggested normality.

'No, my darling, I've slept for long enough. I ought to be arising,' replied Lily.

William moved in close. He took hold of Lily's hips from behind and pulled her near. Her silk gown was soft to his touch. He raised his hand to her cheek and with a finger, brushed aside her hair so that he may press his kiss upon her neck. Before releasing her from his gentle grasp, William wrapped his arms around her, buried his nose deep into her golden locks and sniffed it until his lungs couldn't hold another ounce of breath. He took her hand in his, raised it to his lips and planted a peck of his affection upon it.

His rage could teach the fire how to burn, yet the birds still sang outside his window as if nothing happened here.

William removed himself from Lily's present company to allow her to embrace the day in her own time.

CHAPTER TWENTY-THREE

A Letter for Lily

1 AUGUST, 1913. ALMOST ELEVEN MONTHS LATER.

William was returning from the market and the outside air was as crisp as a blade of grass touched by frost. There was a familiar sense of foreboding in the brittle atmosphere that turned William's stomach.

Before advancing up the stairway to his apartment, William collected the letters that had since gathered in his absence. As he quickly sifted through them, he noticed that one was addressed to Lily.

Marked by an audible sigh, William climbed the stairs.

Lily had awoken in his absence and had since transitioned to the couch, where she sprawled out in her nightgown.

'Good morning, my dear.' William was happy to see her, especially after the oddities he faced with the villagers in the market earlier that day.

Lily didn't respond. She was already occupied, reading from what had looked to William a lot like the parchment on which he would scribe his poetry.

William laid down his shopping and dashed over to Lily to discover she was reading an old piece - his ode to nature.

Somewhat relieved that Lily hadn't found the poem he was deliberately keeping from her, he allowed himself to joke about her looking through his work.

William threw the letters that were still in his hand down beside Lily and began playfully tickling her. She was extremely susceptible to his touch. She creased over in hysterics, rolling about the settee to the ebb and flow of his kind torture.

'Stop! Stop! Look, you're creasing the letters,' squealed Lily through her frenzied laughter.

William broke his tickling and collected the letters that had since packed themselves beneath Lily's leg.

'There's a letter for you,' said William as he offered it to her.

'That's odd,' Lily replied, her face demonstrating her curiosity. 'I never get post here.'

Lily took a moment to study the envelope and the return address on the rear of the packet aided in her inquisitiveness.

'It's from Gran. Of course it is. She's the only one who would write me here.'

William prized the note from her weak grasp and read it to himself, noticing that part of it, the upper corner, had been torn:

My dearest Lily,

I pray life in Mane is treating you well.

It is with regret that I write to you bearing bad news. I have fallen sick and I fear I haven't long left to live. I would like to see you soon and you are welcome to bring someone with you, a friend perhaps? I would feel better knowing you will be safe on your travels.

I had hoped that this letter would find you under better circumstances, but it is important that you know.

Please do not be too troubled by my news. I look forward to your visit.

All my love,
Gran.

P.S. I'm sure Abby will be happy to see you, too.

It wasn't that she hated him, or even fallen out of love with him, just that she couldn't bare the sight of him at that moment.

Lily slammed the bedroom door shut as she exited and made for the front door, with the harsh and painful words, 'Don't expect me back' in place of a passionate goodbye.

William let her go and didn't say a word. He wished he could speak, plead for her to stay, to forgive him already, but he was numb. He just sat on the couch rethinking his behaviour and quickly coming to regret acting in the most brutish and unforgivable way.

CHAPTER TWENTY-FOUR

Lily's Journey East

1 AUGUST, 1909. FOUR YEARS AGO.

Lily boarded the Lanky at four minutes past ten bound for Deadman's Cross, where she would have to change and reset her course further east to Weepers Hollow. A lady of sixty-or-so years of age already occupied her carriage, however, still beset by the argument she had with William that morning, she found comfort in the idea of a travelling companion with whom she could share some light conversation.

The lady was extremely friendly, perhaps overly so. She was incredibly short, so short that her feet barely touched the floor of the carriage. She always held a smile on her face, not the creepy kind, but the kind that told Lily that happiness was all she ever knew.

'Do you mind if I join you?' asked Lily, as she gestured inside the lady's compartment.

'No, no, not at all. Come, sweetheart, come sit.' The lady spoke as if she had never been lonely and Lily felt obligated to match her enthusiasm despite her emotional state.

'My name's Lily,' she said, as she maneuvered into the carriage and took to her seat.

'Hello, Lily. I'm Alice.' There it was again, the smallest of words uttered with the biggest of joy.

She didn't look like an Alice. When heard aloud, Lily thought the name to bear a youthful connotation. And although she was herself once young, Alice's appearance aged, but her name had not.

'Where are you heading?' Lily didn't recognise the lady from the Hollow, neither did Alice recognise Lily. Lily considered that she must have been from one of the neighbouring towns, for the woman's accent was unfamiliar to her.

'I'm travelling to see my daughter. She lives in Beacon Hill. She wrote to me with news of a child.' At last, Lily received some explanation for her constant smile.

'Congratulations,' said Lily, hiding her jealously of her daughter's newborn. 'So you're a grandmother now?' Lily always loved children and always wanted a child of her own. George if it was a boy, Ruby if a girl. She always felt as if there was never the right time to discuss starting a family with William, but how she burned for it.

'Well, I have a son also,' replied Alice. 'His wife gave birth to a baby boy two years ago.' Lily just smiled. 'What about you? Where are you heading?'

'I'm going out to the countryside town of Weepers Hollow to visit my grandmother. She's fallen Ill.' Selfishly, Lily chose to impart her bad news upon the woman who made her feel a little resentment.

'Oh, I'm sorry, my dear. I am so very sorry to hear that.' Even on receipt of Lily's bad news, Alice's smile was still unaltered, her tone upbeat.

'Yes, well, I shall change over at Deadman's Cross. Then on to my hometown.'

'Goodness gracious, you're travelling all that way alone, my dear? Surely a pretty woman like you must have a man in her life to keep her safe and sheltered from life's rain?'

'I do. Yes.' Lily hesitated, as she was reluctant to part with word of her lovers' tiff. 'He was happy for me to go alone.' Instead, she let loose a small gasp of air through her nose and shrugged it off as if putting it down to the unsurprising behaviour of all men. 'I'm sure I'll be fine, though, I know the streets and its people well.'

'Still, you be careful, deary. The nights seem much darker than they used to be.' There was something perturbing in a warning delivered through a gleaming smile. But nonetheless, Lily thanked her for it and for the remainder of their journey together, the women shared casual words and ripe red grapes before Alice disembarked at Beacon Hill.

*

The Lanky arrived at Deadman's Cross the following morning and as Lily crossed the platform, she caught sight of a man. It was the man who gave her grandmother reason to send her away. The sight of him made her shudder and she tried desperately to shield herself from his gaze.

She made it into a new carriage, and in spite of the daylight, quickly drew the drapes. As she peered through the edge of the curtains, her gaze met the man wandering about the platform. As his eyes turned in her direction, Lily sharply retracted her peep. With caution, she returned to looking out of her window to discover the man had removed himself from her view.

The train blew its whistle and began to move out of the station. Lily sank into her chair, pleased of her escape. Her eyes closed as she let out a soft sigh of relief.

As Lily calms, there was a knock at her carriage door. Her ex-lover had found his way to her carriage despite her best efforts at avoiding him.

He was a good-looking man. He possessed a lean physique and was noticeably older than Lily, but only by a few years. He had black hair, slickly arranged upon his perfectly shaped head. He had a charming smile, the same smile that Lily fell for some years ago; but it was a trick, as he was far from charming.

A lump grew in Lily's throat and she was unable to speak. Her limbs froze; they were as hard as the cushioned bench upon which she sat.

'What's the matter, Lily? You don't look too pleased to see me?' he said, mocking her with his tilted head, from which staring out were these psychotic eyes that he wore only for her. 'You don't mind if I join you now, do you?' he said while already pushing through into the carriage. Before Lily could muster any strength of speech to answer, he continued. 'No, of course you don't mind, what a ridiculous question.' As he stepped in, he closed the door behind him, drawing the curtain to the window that looked out into the train's corridor.

'What do you want?' Lily found the energy to speak just a few words and didn't quite fancy wasting them on niceties.

'Now is that a way to greet an old lover? I've been well, thanks for asking.'

'I said, what do you want?' With false daring, she spoke again but a little firmer as if he failed to hear her the first time.

'Lily. Lily. Calm down. There's no need to be getting all…all…worked up. After all, we did share some great times together, didn't we?'

Lily didn't care much for his obnoxious approach. She had no words to return, only a hateful snare.

'Mm! Grapes. I love grapes.' He snatched the bag from the seat beside Lily and helped himself to its contents, throwing the pieces of fruit into his mouth in the most vulgar manner. 'Remember when we used to feed each other grapes beneath the willow tree? It was great times, am I right?' he said, twirling his fingers in a point towards her eyes. 'Yessss, I can see it in your eyes, you remember just fine, girl.' He winked. 'Wait, I've had *the* most brilliant idea. Why don't we pretend that we're back there, beneath the willow tree, you know, where we first…?' He whistled through a licentious grin. 'Hey?' He raised a grape up to her mouth and stared into her eyes with a sudden menace, waiting for her to play along and let him feed her. 'Do you not miss the warmth of my embrace? The weight of me inside of you?'

Lily refused to bow to his will and play his game. She slivered back into the corner of the carriage, repulsed by his very breathing.

Her ex-lover crushed the grape in his fingertips without breaking his intense eye contact.

Lily trembled with fear. She felt vulnerable and she yearned for William.

'What do you want from me?' Lily spoke softly as it was all her voice would allow.

The man suddenly burst out laughing. 'I'm just messing with you,' he said, dismissing his torment of her with a swipe of the air. 'Did I scare you? I didn't mean to scare you.'

There was still something off about the man, something downright ugly governing his intentions.

'Relax. I just want to talk.' He sat back and crossed one leg over the over.

'Talk about what?' Lily didn't trust the man and wasn't about to let her guard down; not until he was out of her sight.

'Well, us, of course.'

'There is no us.'

'See, now that's where I think you're wrong.' The man drew in closer to Lily and lowered his voice so it was little more than a whisper, but a grating one nonetheless. 'You see, I think there is an us, and I'm prepared to take you back, so long as you promise to behave yourself this time and not make me mad. You wouldn't want to make me mad again now, would you?'

'It's over between…' Lily measured her words and spoke firmly, but was cut off by the agitated beast who was sat unpredictable in front of her at an uncomfortably close distance.

'Think carefully before you answer, my sweet.' He ran his hand up the inside of her leg and planted a strong grip upon her naked thigh. Lily detected a threat in his tone and in his fingertips, too, as they pinched into her soft skin. As hard as it was not to surrender to his torment, she remained strong and unmoved.

'I'm in love with another. And even if I wasn't already involved, I would never be yours again.' Lily spoke her mind freely but was frightened to the core by what his response might be. In a bold outburst, she spat in his face; she didn't want him to sense her fear, as that's when predators thrive the most.

For a moment, which felt for Lily like a millennium, the man remained stoic; he was intense, unflinching, an embodiment of evil like a statue of Hades himself. She could see the tension in his jaw as he gritted his teeth.

'OK! Alright. I get it,' he said, snapping into action and wiping his face of her spit. He then pulled himself away from her. 'Well, it was nice seeing you again, Lily. I take it you're heading to the Hollow, so perhaps I'll see you around.'

Lily detected a hidden threat in that; a threat that was confirmed when he blew her a kiss, as there was nothing at all romantic or cheeky about it, just plain evil.

As he left, there was a stir in his eyes, a look that was unsettling and which would stay with Lily for days to come. As he removed himself from her carriage, Lily began to sob quietly to herself, disgusted by the man's touch and deeply unsettled by the experience.

CHAPTER TWENTY-FIVE

Left Behind

20 AUGUST, 1909. TWENTY DAYS AFTER LILY LEFT.

Although William had lived alone before, everything felt strange without Lily and in her absence, the only place he could find a reasonable degree of relief from the gut-wrenching pain of solitude was sat at his writing desk, scribing his thoughts before attempting to mould them into either letters to Lily or works of respectable literature.

If he fell short of inspiration, which he often did, he would find it in a photograph he kept of his parents. There was something in the photo that grabbed William's attention each time he glanced at it. His mother was wearing a ring for which in the middle was held a round diamond that sparkled in every imaginable colour.

The days were difficult, but bearable. It was the nights that troubled him the most. All the times that he spent just laying awake in bed gazing into nothing and feeling detached from everything and everyone.

Stung by guilt's tail, William was held in hurt's wake and felt numb from head to toe.

As he sat alone by the fire, he was reminded of the vacancies that his lover drew there. He felt trapped in the space between happiness and hardness, free of her presence and laughter.

William detached himself from his self-pity and twisted a gaze out the window. Amidst the darkened plume were stars that shone brightly.

Under the same set of stars, we lay worlds apart was William's lasting thought as his dreams came in to carry him away.

CHAPTER TWENTY-SIX

An Apology

SEVEN DAYS AFTER LILY LEFT.

7 AUGUST, 1909

Lily,

How could I be so stupid? To let you slip away like that without the reassurance that I love you - that I would do anything for you. I was blind and already I hate myself for it. You were right; I should have come with you. Write to me. Tell me you're safe and that you forgive me so I may receive some peace of mind.

I pray all is well with you and your grandmother.

Until I see you again, my love x

Days later, William's letter arrived at Riddle Manor. However, it was delivered into the hands of Lily's grandmother, who had only recently been made aware of William's existence and his behaviour.

Gran was extremely protective over Lily and the thought of William allowing her to travel alone made her blood boil; especially after hearing of the vile turn of events that Lily faced on her train journey.

Lily was in the town catching up with familiar folk and her grandmother showed no hesitation in invading her privacy and reading William's letter.

As she gave reading to his plea, she grew angrier. The way his words sought forgiveness for his own wellbeing crawled under her skin and reminded her of the good she was doing in keeping her from the selfishness and cruelty of men. She begrudged menfolk so much that she looked only upon the bad in them, and it never occurred to her that William may have been different if only she gave him the chance.

Thinking she knew what was best for her granddaughter, the lady threw the letter upon the fire and spoke nothing of it.

She even managed to talk Lily out of writing to William. Although she was concerned for her lover and surprised that he hadn't made contact already, Lily didn't see why she should be the one to give in, to show herself to be weak. No. She was stronger than that.

CHAPTER TWENTY-SEVEN

A Night to Forget

1 SEPTEMBER, 1909. THIRTY-TWO DAYS AFTER LILY LEFT.

Lily walked the sinister streets of her hometown with conviction while nervously looking around her. She was familiar with every inch of paving that lay beneath her feet, unchanged from when she was a little girl.

Through a gate, she veered left away from the village and headed across the grassland that lead up the hill. All was as dark and quiet as a grave, spooky too, but Lily felt empowered by treading home soil.

Breaching the silence was the sound of twigs snapping, but Lily's strides were tiny and her footsteps soft, not the kind that would cause such audible crunches. She stopped dead in her tracks and strained her ears. She heard, again, the breaking of wood nearby and she knew that she wasn't alone. Sick with the feeling of fear, she turned, only to be clubbed to the ground in a single swipe.

Lily lay dazed and face down in the mud. Before she could fully regain her senses, she felt her attacker climb on her back.

The moon adjusted its gaze and cast a spotlight upon Lily's panic-stricken face as if for the world to see; everything else was selfishly kept in darkness.

Crows, as black as the night and the act to come, perched on the treetops above, the only witnesses, gawking as if receiving some sick pleasure from Lily's dehumanisation.

The man, and it was a man judging by the strength he bore, pulled out a knife and pressed the cool steel edge upon Lily's cheek in an attempt to hush her cries. In that, her sobbing was reduced, yet audible still – resonating somehow.

The violence scared Lily and reminded her of how William would often scare her in his flurries of aggression when he had forgotten himself. In relationships, she was rather used to dealing with violence, but nothing of this nature. There was something hypnotic in her beauty that turned men into animals, and sometimes she even blamed herself, a victim of her own attraction.

Beneath the man's body, Lily trembled with alarm. He carved a tiny gash into her soft cheek to stir his pleasure;

such perfection marred by jealously like Michelangelo staining the Mona Lisa.

Frightened for her life, Lily submitted to the will of the knife and all of a sudden, every shred of conviction, every shred of empowerment, suddenly drained from her body like water from a wrung cloth. She felt cold. Removed. She longed for William and suddenly regretted running off like that.

He lowered the knife to her throat and as she lay with her cheek in the dirt, his other hand slid down her side to rip away her clothing just enough for him to pass.

He took firm hold of her breasts and felt himself grow tall like the grass beneath his knees.

With her own torn clothing, he blindfolded Lily as if she wasn't already cut off from the world. She felt detached. Her earth suddenly went black. All other senses were heightened: the touch of him poking around inside of her; the smell of her own blood as it fused with the ugly smell of his sweat in the air around them; the taste of the dirt and disconnect as it filled her mouth and the grating sound of his piggish grunts.

Lily was alone and she succumbed to the act of brutality only to ease the pain of the struggle. Like a ragdoll, her body pulsed in the mud to the ebb and flow of his penetration.

'Why are you doing this to me?' cried Lily through her tears and torment. But he was cold and unresponsive. If anything, her pleading seemed to heighten his pleasure.

As he grew into his rhythm, he pushed Lily's face deeper into the ground. He arched his back to achieve a greater thrust. With each stroke, Lily's body became even more limp.

Lily's breath came in short, sharp bursts; her fingers clawed deep into the dirt.

The time between each stab grew shorter. Her body whimpered. His body contracted. Then stillness. After just minutes that felt for Lily like hours, the predator reached crescendo, as his seed surged down his shaft.

As her attacker reached his tainted release inside of her, he buried his nose deep into her golden hair and sniffed it, allowing her perfumed scent to fuse with the sensations of climaxing.

Just moments from her grandmother's home, Lily lay flaccid and disgraced. No longer possessing the energy to cry, she focused on gathering her breathing, steadying it so.

Again, the rage turned inside of the aggressor and, with the butt-end of his knife, he bashed her skull until his hands morphed into the colour of her blood.

'I'm sorry,' he shouted as if he had no choice but to drive the handle of his blade into her beautiful crown. 'I'm sorry,' he continued, as if it would make any difference to the woman whose life had been cut short.

He wept like a child at his act of cold-hearted cruelty. He stared at his stained hands as if they weren't his own. He removed her blindfold and his body began to shake as he peeled himself away from Lily's corpse and shuffled back into the shelter of the night.

With each cry he grew louder, almost as if he was giving noise to Lily's pain, too. The moonlight turned away, almost in disgust, and left them in the total darkness.

CHAPTER TWENTY-EIGHT

Another Letter

FOURTEEN DAYS AFTER LILY LEFT.

14 AUGUST, 1909

Lily,

I am yet to receive word of your safety and my imagination is torturing me with all sorts of morbid 'what ifs'. I understand that you must still be wounded by my behaviour, but I beg you, lay to rest those tribulations long enough to send a reply so I may stop worrying.

I am tired, Lily. I haven't slept a decent night since you left. In your absence, I've been reminded of how much I truly do love you and if anything happened to you, I would lose my mind. Not being there to protect you would destroy me.

I pray you haven't fallen out of love with me, or in love with another, because of my insensitive actions. Bless me with one more chance, as without you, I am nothing, just a shadow of a man that once was.

Until I see you again, my love x

Days later, William's letter arrived at Riddle Manor. However, it was delivered into the hands of Lily's grandmother.

Thinking she knew what was best for her granddaughter, she threw the letter upon the fire and spoke nothing of it.

CHAPTER TWENTY-NINE

Tears of the Hollow

6 SEPTEMBER, 1909. THIRTY-SEVEN DAYS AFTER LILY LEFT.

On this day, Weepers Hollow wore a frown, as the entire village turned out for Lily's laying to rest. All around the church were saddened faces; even the sky bore a grim expression.

Everybody shared a familiar drabness in outfit and filling the crowd were those who shed tears, those who kept themselves together and those who were clearly just there out of neighbourly obligation.

Nonetheless, the Hollow turned out its pockets of people and the service was as populated as it could have been, with the exception of William, of course, who clearly hadn't received detail of Lily's passing and who could not be reached in the several dormant days that separated her death and committal.

Stood amongst the rally of villagers was Lily's grandmother. She was a spindly old woman, clearly suffering from some kind of disease of the flesh, most of which was masked by her formal attire. Her eyes were sore from tireless weeping and her hair, greyed in colour, was neatly arranged upon her head. She was wrinkled, but her age was good to her. It was a wonder how long it would last, however, as her body already showed signs of corrosion.

As she shook hands in receipt of people's condolences, she trembled under the weight and uneasiness of her position.

Lead by Lily's grandmother, the mourners entered into the holy embrace of the church and took to the pews. Heavy was the woman's heart who had lost her grandaughter while acting upon her invitation; despite knowing better, Gran blamed herself for the tragedy.

She sobbed profoundly at the sight of Lily's coffin, resting at the end of the aisle beneath a statue of Jesus Christ as if her body was an offering to him, a sacrifice of some kind.

The priest poised beyond the alter receiving his flock and ready to deliver the ceremony.

He was a particularly short man, stood only five feet tall and was dwarfed even more so by his baggy, but rather colourful garments when in comparison to that of his audience. He wore white with purple highlights and the colour was quite refreshing amongst the sea of black and grey. He might have been anywhere between fifty-five and seventy years of age, with a flatness and formality of manner that revealed nothing at all of his own personality.

Even after all was seated and silent - bar that of suppressed weeping - the priest remained quiet for a moment still.

The sermon itself was brief and was constructed of a few hymns, pieces of poetry and various readings of a religious nature. After, the church emptied out into the graveyard in anticipation of the burial.

On either side and away in the near distance stood the gravestones. But in front was a freshly dug trench which was to house Lily in her casket. As the coffer was lowered, the priest gave a final reading, which speckled the atmosphere with further solemnity:

> *'For as much as it hath contented Almighty God of his great forgiveness to take unto himself the soul of our beloved sister here departed, we, therefore, commit her body to the ground; earth to earth, ashes to ashes, dust to dust...'*

A select few, those who desired to pay their last respects, approached the grave to drop a flower upon her casket and to give gesture and voice to their more intimate blessings.

A kind villager of a younger standing aided Lily's grandmother, frail in her ill condition, in the afternoon's affair, while kept her reasonable company during the wake, which was held in The Slaughters Barrel.

The Barrel welcomed the whole of the Hollow through its doors this day and as the evening grew old, word of William fell from the grandmother's grief and was passed from lip to lip like genes through generations.

CHAPTER THIRTY

He's Coming

TWENTY-EIGHT DAYS AFTER LILY LEFT.

28 AUGUST, 1909

Lily,

My mind is now but a spectre of the macabre, plagued by dark eventualities in your neglect of me. I have spent many nights watching the space that grows between us and I scratch at the scabs of my conscience. I have tried my best to embrace the bleakness in which I bathe, but I cannot live any longer without being reassured of your safety; it brings me great concern that I am yet to hear from you. This can't be it for us. The guilt lays heavy on this soul of mine and I am breaking up without you by my side. I need to see you. I need to know that I haven't lost you forever. I'm coming.

I will be journeying to Weepers Hollow on Friday, 30 August, taking the four minutes past ten train from Mane travelling around the Marsh Land via Deadman's Cross and up through Holmwood Forrest. I expect it will take me a few days, a little longer perhaps, as I am unversed in travel and all I have is the address to find you. But I will find you, and I eagerly wait the day that I am to be with you once more.

Until I see you again, my love x

Days later, William's letter arrived at Riddle Manor. However, it was delivered into the hands of Lily's grandmother.

Thinking she knew what was best for her granddaughter, she threw the letter upon the fire and spoke nothing of it.

She prayed that he would not fulfil his intentions. However, should the day come when William landed on her doorstep, she was to claim, with cunning, that no letters had arrived.

CHAPTER THIRTY-ONE

The Way Back Again

2 SEPTEMBER, 1913. PRESENT DAY.

The world, once so light and full of promise, was reduced to a mere reminder of what William doesn't have, can never have again, and didn't have for long enough.

William retreated from his plans in fear of there being a witness to what he was about to do.

'Evening, Willy Boy,' declared Garrick on approach, and in his usual, distinctive voice.

'Good Evening to you, Stanley,' replied William, through an audible sigh.

'What were you looking at, boy?' asked Garrick in the most curious manner, as he attempted to trace William's gaze. 'All I can see is our reflections in the grocery shop window.'

'Apologies. It has been rather a long day and my mind is far from meeting.'

'Well climb up, boy, let Troy take you there?' said Garrick, holding out a hand. 'Looks like you could do with a rest.'

A little under forty minutes later, they arrived at Weepers Hollow Station where Garrick left William to go about his journey home.

William settled in the carriage and embraced the notion of being homebound.

He pulled a flat peak cap from his sack and lowered it over his brow, which, if nothing else, gave him a place to hide from the streetlamps that burned through the carriage window.

He put his weary feet up and had no qualms in saying goodnight to the day that lead him there.

In his sleep, William dreamt an old dream of Lily lying limp on a bed of blood while the cold darkness closed in around her. William moved in to kneel down beside her and as he did so, Lily awoke from her death to smile up at him.

In the dream, Riddle Manor lurked in the near distance. The interior lights were on and the house looked a pleasant place, despite its isolation.

'It's you. It was always you,' Lily whispered to William through the smile that used to hypnotise him and remind him of how lucky he was.

As she spoke, tears fell from William's eyes. He took Lily's hand in his, and, as he did so, they filled with blood. Stunned, he dropped Lily's hands with haste and leapt back in horror.

He closed his eyes ready to wake up, but each time they opened, his scene grew more and more torturous.

This time, he was holding a knife stained with the colour red. He looked to Lily, but her beauty had mutated into something quite hideous. The flesh had wasted away around her face and all he saw was the whiteness of bone, marred by the remains of stale skin yet to erode.

William's gaze was swallowed up in the black holes that were once the most magnificent set of eyes. The dark spaces captured his attention and, as he felt himself getting sucked into them, he awoke from his nightmare, sweating and screaming.

'No! No!' he shrieked, until he realised it was but a dream.

As he sat up, gripping his head and calming it, he heard voices that began to haunt him like a montage in his head - voices that he remembered from his days of future past.

'Two slabs of my prime steak *again* is it, sir?'

'Indeed it is.'

'*You* did that to her.'

'Find your peace, William, and don't come back next time.'

'Of course you do…who *doesn't* know that man?'

'*Screams*…sir?'

'Heading home so soon?'

'I've learned to expect that sort of thing.'

'All I can see is our reflections.'

'Whenever you need me, I'll be there.'

'Until next time.'

The lie that William burrowed deep in his soul was suddenly naked for his eyes to see. It brought a nasty and sour taste that lingered in his mouth - it was the taste of guilt and wild delusions.

The voices carried him to the realisation of what he had done and the puzzle that plagued his mind was whole once more.

CHAPTER THIRTY-TWO

The Man in My Footsteps

William was disturbed by the faintest of sounds emanating from his bedroom.

With a knife in his clutches, he gingerly approached his bedroom door, which was already ajar, and gently pressed a hand to it.

As he slowly swung the door open, there stood Lily in her nightgown, looking into her hand mirror and fixing her make-up.

William immediately dropped the knife.

He moved in close. He took hold of Lily's hips from behind and pulled her near. Her silk gown was soft to his touch. He raised his hand to her cheek and with a finger, brushed aside her hair so that he may press his kiss upon her neck. He wrapped his arms around her, buried his nose deep into her golden locks and sniffed it until his lungs couldn't hold another ounce of breath.

As he pulled away, he caught his own reflection, trapped as it were in Lily's mirror. He gave himself a look. It was the kind of look that you only give to your enemy when you know that one of you must die.

William let Lily go from his grasp and he walked towards the door.

After just a few paces, he stopped.

'You know, I wonder,' said William as the sun pressed its glow upon the left side of his face.

'What's that, Eddy?' replied Lily, as she fixed her sweet gaze upon him.

He gently turned back to face Lily. He stayed silent for a moment just watching her. His glazed and intense stare gave away his troubled soul, but there was a glimmer of hope in it yet.

Then again he spoke: 'Which is worse: to live in a lie, or to die embracing the truth?'

He walked out, letting the door shut behind him.

THE END

To you, my friend,

Let me tell you a secret, but promise you'll keep it between you and me: a man is really a fickle child in disguise. When he moves forward, he finds loss and he fears what he found.

When that day came for me - the day when my world collapsed like it will for you - there were things that I never asked her, but how they ruin me now. I scrambled over faces and clambered over walls trying to reach the pure sky, but ahead there was just darkness and everything behind me had died.

Some advice for you now: come in from the callous confines of your mind, because guilt is all you'll find there and guilt is wasteful. Guilt was my poison that brewed in the obscurity of my perception. But for you, tomorrow will come, and tomorrow may well bring the sunshine again.

As you walked with me, I stumbled through the years, one day to the next, caught in the gap between rapture and damnation. In a forgotten reality traced unto a dream, I saw myself sin. I ran through the vacant passages of my mind and hid in the darkest corner of my soul, just to keep the fire from burning within.

It's true that I built a world with her love and I built it in me.

The past is the grubby air contained in a sealed box, forever swirling, changing, rocked by the passing of time and my would-be thoughts. The past is also very seldom as we would have it and although our view of it may alter, it can never be erased. The future? Now there we have choices, and now that the tempest has settled, I must make mine.

The noose is slack still, yet I can feel already the fibres of rope tighten against my neck, the air deplete from my lungs. I admit it's a familiar feeling and one that may culminate in peace at last.

Turn your gaze. You don't need to see this.

But before you leave, let me ask you something: once you poison the body, how do you ever get it out of the bloodstream?

Now go. Break free from this nightmare and see it your way. I'll take the long way 'round.

Yours faithfully,
William Hardy

Take to burden
Your broken soul,
You built it up
To one day feel whole.
But now the fragments
Are fighting back,
You surrender to delusion
And trust a pretend attack.

Dreams become nightmares,
Nightmares become reality,
What's left to do but
To give in to mortality.
I have a choice
I know I do,
But the man in my footsteps
Wants to see this all through.

Trapped in the dark
With no light to see,
Trapped in my mind
With no way to break free.
Where there's a way
There is my will,
A lie will hurt
But the truth will kill.

A Note from the Author

I hope you enjoyed reading my debut gothic thriller. Your support of my work is massively appreciated and I wish I could thank you all individually.

If at this point you find yourself a little perplexed, you may find, like some of my other readers, that a second pass will help to provide clarity. Knowing how the story ends, you'll pick up on many hidden clues and hopefully find pleasure and satisfaction in piecing together the puzzle; after all, it's no bad thing to have to work at a novel.

If you have any burning questions about this, or indeed my wider work, I'm always happy to speak to my readers so why not connect with me via my social media channels.

Sincerely,

Anthony

Twitter: @byAnthonyLowery
Facebook: /byAnthonyLowery

Lightning Source UK Ltd.
Milton Keynes UK
UKHW040636310319
340217UK00001B/69/P